WHAT

WOULD

I DO

WITHOUT

YOU?

A collection of s[...]
about frien[...]

MARGO T KRASNE

To my beloved niece Nancy Weisberg

who once asked me,

"How do you make friends?"

My question:

"How do you keep them?"

Then there was my incredible friend Janet Riccio

who showed me how.

They both will be remembered forever.

Table of Contents

Introduction to Friends

"No one needs to know our business—nor yours for that matter!" my mother used to say. Yet from the earliest age, whether out of a desperate need to be understood, or simply as a means to connect with another person on more than a surface level, the line between what could reasonably be shared and that which should be kept to oneself, I constantly crossed. I felt compelled to let those around me know what I was experiencing—whether it be resentment for something done to me, or guilt about something I had done to another. Thankfully, I did have enough sense to subscribe to the theory that no one person should be privy to it all.

Later in life, as a communications coach, I would share my own embarrassing moments made in front of audiences—and the fact I had survived—to help clients put to bed their own fears of speaking in public. Then, as I neared my eighties, I exposed myself even more in a memoir. One reader reacting as my mother would have. "Oh my God!" her husband could hear her gasp from the next room, "Why is she telling the world all of this?"

I'm telling *you* this, because when I decided to write about the various friendships I've had—in all their complexities, what maintained or destroyed them, the commonality that dissipated when lives changed, when misunderstandings piled up until the friendship collapsed under their weight—I assumed my thoughts would spill easily out onto the page. And at first it seemed they would. I'd start off with a great opening paragraph, one I so delighted in, I'd call a friend to share. Then I'd hang up and watch the rest of the page remain empty for hours if not days. Sometimes I even made it to the bottom of a page before something would stop me from moving ahead. It was as if one part of my brain had all this material that was dying to flow forth while another part worked beaver-like at building a dam to prevent one word from getting through.

Then it dawned. It was one thing to expose my imperfections, but another's? How does one do that without muddying all concerned? It was only when I gave myself permission to write each story as it had unfolded that I could identify the underlying truth of the relationship. Once I had that, I could decide whether to take its essence and create a whole new scenario (much like the writer does in Starlight Starbright,) fictionalize it enough so that privacy of others was protected, or tell it as it had happened which I did in three: *Gigi and Me, Lotte and I,* and *Dead Daisies Strewn All Over.*

No matter how the various friendships played out, I am so very grateful they existed.

Margo T Krasne

Like Sisters

They knew each other's likes, dislikes. Admired each other's strong points and accepted the other's weaknesses. Their friendship made all the more fluid due to the one's compulsion to lead, and the other's proclivity to leaving the decision making to her friend.

They spoke almost daily. Saw each other at a minimum twice a month. Would go with the other to a worrisome doctor's appointment taking notes as the doctor explained the diagnosis or discussed a procedure. And they would sit together in wait for a veterinarian's pronouncement as to whether the one's dog or the other's cat would live. Whatever the verdict they would be there for each other whether to console or to celebrate. Sisters. Always.

There were differences of course. One was married. Had been twice. The other single with a stream of affairs in her wake. And like sisters they didn't always agree. One preferred to attend pop concerts or the latest hit movie, the other obscure foreign films and experimental off-Broadway plays. But the differences only made the friendship more interesting. And while one took enormous pleasure in shopping and acquiring items that delighted her eyes—"I earned it; I can spend it!"— the other worried about spending even a penny over her unnecessarily strict budget. Her disapproval as to her friend's spreading habits often more than apparent by her hard to miss roll of the eyes.

Of course, over time, hurt feelings were unavoidable. *"You had no right telling them what I said." "You never said it was a secret." "Anything I tell you is a secret unless I say otherwise!"*

And because they knew each other so well, too well some would say, they knew just where to find the other's weak spots. *"Oh, for God's sake. Stop complaining about your weight and get thee to a gym!" "Well, maybe if you'd stop judging me with your own eating disordered mind, I'd be able to."*

Still, for years, twelve to be exact, after sometimes brief, sometimes unbearably long separations—the time it could take for a wound to heal—they would find a way back. To their friendship. Their sisterhood. They found their way back after a raucous, even slightly ridiculous political debate over whether or not there'd been WMDs. *"It was idiotic to believe they existed." "Are you calling me an idiot?"* They found their way back after Ms. Frugal quipped *"No, I didn't understand how you could spend thousands of dollars on your dog just to give him a few more months." "I spent it because if there was an outside chance that he'd have a few more years, I wanted him to have them. Or is it that you're so damn tight you'd let Mischmisch die?"*

They even found their way back after, *"Hey you two, please stop bickering, please. It's painful to watch." "Then leave! You know nothing about relationships— your longest being what? A few months?"*

They kept finding their way back until the day one called to say she needed company while she looked for a pair of boots, and the other said, *"I don't think you need me for that."* A benign interaction so weighty that neither woman had the strength to pick up the phone and call the other ever again.

Star Light Star Bright

Liz (Lisa)
Jeri (Jane)
Mrs. M (Mrs. M for now)
Billy Diamond (Bill Damon)
Mike (Mitch)

Two weeks before Mrs. M at 57 climbed onto the windowsill, she'd hurled the frying pan she'd planned to use for the Lyonnaise potatoes across the room at her 84-year-old mother. ~~She missed and the pan clipped the ear of Mrs. M's daughter Lisa's best friend Jane. All the old woman had~~ *All the old woman had done was to suggest Mrs. M turn down the light under the pot on the stove and just like that Jane watched the woman she considered to be the perfect mom morph into a catapult of rage. The pan missed Mrs. M's mom but clipped Jane's ear as she tried to shield the old lady. Two weeks later in the presence of her husband and daughter, Mrs. M strode through the room, not looking right nor left, opened the window, and stepped off into oblivion from the 19th floor. Mrs. M had no idea that moments before her own mother,* ~~at whom Mrs. M's anger was actually directed~~*, had left the room to prepare dinner in the kitchen, diluting. . .*

Jeri rubbed her left earlobe—something she did mindlessly whenever deep in thought—though in this instance it was more like deep in a polemical battle with herself. Why had she ever acquiesced to Liz's, "Swear you'll never write about this!" hissed under her breath, as they stood beside Mrs. M's coffin? Liz's rage so palpable that Jeri worried Liz would begin pounding on it in an attempt to rouse Mrs. M from the dead. Her "I mean it, Jeri! Swear on your life—or better yet, your mother's life. Yes, your mom's life, swear!" Words that reverberated in Jeri's head to this day. And Jeri had sworn. She never wrote about how Liz's father called rabbi after rabbi looking for one who would perform a service over a suicide. Never put to paper how eventually he found one who would agree to officiate but only if he could portray Mrs. M as being mentally ill. And, she had never used in any one of her stories Liz's classical utterance: "Why the hell should I go? She walked out on us, didn't she?" In all the years when Jeri couldn't pull a creative thread from her brain to unravel another story, when she knew Liz's mom's death was there for the picking, had she gone back on her word? No! A promise was a promise, and she wasn't going to risk losing her best friend over her own limitations as a writer. That is, until now. Sixteen years after the fact.

But what choice did she have? Until recently only two of her stories had been published and those in obscure literary magazines. But then, on a whim, she submitted one she had little hope for and voila! it won her not only a $1500 prize, but the possibility of an agent. No contract or anything like that. But an agent who, after reading several of Jeri's stories suggested she write one long one. "Short story collections are a bitch to sell," the agent had said. "But if it contains one that's almost of novella length, well . . ." And Jeri had cut the agent off with, "No problem. Understood. Will get on it," completely disregarding the obvious—that she would need to write a story with at least 10,000 more words than her usual count of around 5000.

Still, she would not now be going back on her word if the brain jam that followed hadn't been one of the worst she'd ever experienced. Everyday she'd come home from her job, grab something from the fridge, pour a large glass of wine and head for the computer—and nothing. Not one bloody word. She'd even taken a week of vacation days assuming concentrated time would unleash her creative powers. Pages upon pages filled with nothing but doodles. Distraught, she booked a session with her old therapist who, after listening to Jeri's all too often repeated plaint, asked one of those typical shrink-y questions. "Do you think this could have to do with your dying to write about Liz's mom and that promise of yours?"

"No! Of course not!" Jeri had snapped. "Besides, you know I'm forbidden to write about that!"

"But you've wanted to write about it for as long as I've known you. And there's enough there to probably get you to the required length. Correct?"

Jeri reached for the tissues as her tears began. "Liz was there for me all through my mom's death. Never once brought up the difference of our losses. Not once. And she could have. She certainly could have."

"True. You both have been good friends to each other. But there are things you've withheld. Why not keep this from her until you've finished. Better yet, keep it to yourself until it has been accepted by a publisher."

"Just thinking about writing it without her permission, turns my stomach."

"So, let me get this straight. You're blocked. You need a story for the agent. Liz's would make a good one, but you believe you can't write it without her permission which you're convinced you cannot get. Sounds like you've boxed yourself in. Might as well call the agent and explain that you have given up writing."

Jeri couldn't move. The idea of never writing again twisted every fiber in her body. And then, she heard the magic words. Words her shrink had never uttered before.

"Jeri, has it ever dawned on you that Liz—with all the therapy she's had—could be okay with the story being told. A lot of time has passed. Have you thought about that? Not that I think you should test the waters until it's finished. *And* accepted. But . . ."

Jeri left the therapist's office resolved to shove her guilt to the side. To write and keep it to herself. Why, she thought, she might even become a better writer if she put her words directly to paper rather than letting them fly from her mouth into the air where they could get diluted. Yes, that is what she'd do. As soon as she got home.

In the end, Lisa did attend her mother's funeral. She begged ~~Jeri~~ Jane to stay close at all times. And Jane complied even though she would have preferred to sit way in the back off by herself. She too had suffered a loss. Mrs. M had been her confidant, her mentor, the woman to whom she ran when interactions at her own home became untenable. She cringed at Lisa's loud snorts when the rabbi described Mrs. M as a "woman of valor." She pretended she didn't hear Lisa's "Like hell it was" when the rabbi added that Mrs. M's "price was above riches," and she slid way down in her seat when Lisa stood up and told the rabbi that he was the crazy one after he ended with "let us pray that she is now released from the madness that overtook her."

The Shiva that followed the interment was even weirder what with all the liquor and food laid out on the dining table giving the impression of a festive occasion rather than a ritual of mourning. Add Bill Damon, Lisa's high school crush, to the mix who showed up with a guy he'd just met at a bar and . . .

Jeri jumped up and headed to the kitchen to reheat her coffee. No reason to write about the sex she'd had with Billy Diamond in the car ride home. Especially since she'd never told Liz. Not that Liz could have held it against her considering she'd glommed onto Billy's friend making it clear to all that she was probably taking him to her bed that very night. No, Liz thought as she headed back to her desk, the cab ride could be left out. Not part of the story.

Jeri wondered what it would be like to have enough money, so she no longer had to don work attire and head to an office. Not have to spend her days editing ad copy for OTC meds. Simply to be able to walk around the house, coffee in hand, thinking of what she should or should not write next. Like perhaps something about how sexual desire often accelerates after weddings and burials.

~~Six months later, with his wife gone, her mother now ensconced in a home for the aged, and his married to Mitch, Mr. M found himself free of all encumbrances and took advantage of such by~~

The phone range and mindlessly Jeri picked it up. "Yes?"

"Guess who died?"

"What?"

"Oh, for Christ's sake. Good morning, Jeri—though it's more like afternoon. Guess who died."

Jeri checked the clock. It was after 12. She had blissfully lost track of time.

"I said, guess!" Liz repeated.

"Guess what?"

"Liz to Jeri, guess who died?"

"Who?"

"Billy Diamond. Can you imagine? 37 and gone! Just like that. It's in the Times."

"You're kidding? I was just. . . "Jeri stopped herself.

"Just what?"

"No, nothing. Crazy."

"You were about to say something. You were just what?"

Jeri tried to escape, "I was just thinking about when we were kids and then you call and tell me about Billy. Was he married?"

"Says to a Jennie Evans. Two kids. So, are you planning to write about us?"

"You and Billy?"

"No, you and me."

"I am not planning to write about us!" It wasn't a total lie. At this point she didn't know where the story would take her.

"Jeri, listen. Trust me, you'll find something to write about. You've had blocks before. Maybe stop trying so hard. Give it a break. I have an idea. I'm thinking of paying a condolence call, come with me."

"When was the last time you thought of Billy Diamond?"

"I think of him . . . sometimes. Besides I knew his parents. They must be devastated. So, come with me."

"No!" Jeri said a bit too emphatically. "You go. Liz, listen, I've got to get back to work."

"Hah! So, you have started a new piece. Well keep at it. 10,000 words, here we come!"

"I'm just playing with ideas. Talk later. Okay?" Jeri hung up fast. One minute more and she'd have confessed.

Even though the girls had gone to the same school since 1st grade, their friendship didn't really take hold until they were sent to the same summer camp and Lisa, having gone the summer before, was assigned the task of "looking out for the newbie." A perfect pairing. Lisa by far the more outgoing, Jane more reticent to engage. 'Popular by proximity' Jane would later describe it—Lisa's friends accepting Jane simply because Lisa did . . .

"Look!" Lisa cried one evening outside their bunk.

Jane followed Lisa's finger up until her eyes rested on the only visible star.

"Ready?"

"Ready! Three, two, one!"

"Starlight starbright, first star I see tonight

Wish I may, wish I might, have the wish I wish tonight."

It was a ritual that would get repeated summer after summer. Stars rarely visible in the city.

"What did you wish for?" Lisa demanded.
"You know I can't tell, or it won't come true."

"Then what if we both tell each other and promise to keep it a secret. It would be our rules."

"Okay, but then you have to tell me yours. Promise?"

"Promise! I wished," Lisa whispered," that Billy Diamond would ask me to go steady."

"Billy Diamond?" Jane exclaimed, surprised at Lisa's choice. "Really?

"Really! Cross your heart and hope to die you won't tell."

"Cross my heart and hope to die."

"Now tell me yours," Lisa demanded.

"I wished I will become a famous writer."

And just as Jeri thought she had moved forward with the story; a wave of guilt overtook her, and she began crossing out line after line.

"We have to talk," she blurted out when Liz picked up.

"And good morning to you."

"Sorry. But we have to."

"So, talk!"

"In person."

"My God! You're dying."

"No, of course not. Nothing like that."

"Then spill!"

And like a speeding train with no space between its cars, Jeri began to apologize profusely without saying for what. Then she reminded Liz of the agent's request for a longer story to add to the collection and how blocked she'd been, "You know I haven't been able to get a word down. Even went back to Dr. B." Finally, she slowed down and, in a voice pleading for understanding and forgiveness, she confessed, "You, us, your mom's story just cried to come out, Liz. It's been sitting there. Waiting. The more I pushed it away, the more blocked I became. Liz, I promise. Promise! I will camouflage everything, but I can't write this without you knowing." She held her breath. "Liz?" And the phone went dead.

Jeri tried calling, but Liz wouldn't answer the phone. She wrote email after email to no effect. "Liz won't talk to me," she told various friends in hopes they would intercede. But all she got back was, "Give it time," or "I'm sure this will pass" or "You guys have been friends way too long to have this come between you." She returned to Dr. B who tried a new tack. "It is your story as well, Jeri. I mean you do have a jagged ear to prove it."

Ever so slowly Jeri found her desire for Liz's absolution replaced by small geysers of rage. How could Liz deprive her of the possibility of success? Liz who was working her way up the corporate ladder, bonuses increasing by the year, while she, Jeri, had to work at a mediocre paying job just so she could have her nights and weekends free to write. It wasn't as if she was expecting a best seller that would allow her total freedom. But perhaps a bit more ease? No, she'd let Liz keep her punitive silence and she, Jeri, would write the story.

It took a few more weeks for Jeri get it all down. The speed with which all the changes in the M family's life had occurred. The woman who, as rumor had it, Mr. M had been seeing on the side for years, moving in with him. Liz's marriage to Mitch and the way she made sure she spent as much of her father's money as possible on the wedding, the divorce that followed, and Liz's worrisome depression. Jeri even included her cab ride home with Billy as well as her own mother's death—not that she hadn't written about her mother many times before, but this version had all to do with the way Liz had mourned Jeri's mom as if she'd been her own.

Once the past in all its detail had found its way to the page, Jeri began again with new names that bore no resemblance to Mrs. M, Liz, or anyone else. She altered appearances. Gave each an entirely different personality, even added a younger brother to the mix, so that the people Jeri had based the story on were now unrecognizable even to her. She placed the family in the dining room at a Thanksgiving dinner. Had the mother walk into the room with the turkey, set the platter in front of her husband, hand him the carving knife, then walk to the window as if to allow air into the room before climbing up and out. Jeri titled it 'Thanksgiving' and used the not so original device of each character relating the story from his or her perspective beginning with the mother's rant and ending (at 976 words) with her painful regret as she fell.

It took three months for the story to take enough shape for Jeri to feel confident it worked and another three to feel she'd nailed it. She emailed a copy to the agent and one to Liz. That Liz might delete it without reading, well, so be it.

A few weeks later, the agent called to say a publisher was interested. Nothing definite, but a definite possibility. Jeri emailed Dr. B to say thanks. Then she waited.

The caller id showed Liz's number. Jeri held her breath and answered.

"I read it."

"And?"

"Do you think that's what mom thought?"

"Well, there was a TV program about suicides off the Golden Gate bridge and the few who had survived the jump, all said they'd regretted stepping off the moment they had." Jeri waited through the silence that followed.

"What are you doing tomorrow?" Liz said.

"Working, but from home. Why?"

"Have a doc appointment, want to come with me?"

"For?"

"Tell you tomorrow."

"What time? I'll work it out."

At 11 the next morning they waited in the oncologist's office.

"Scared?" Jeri whispered.

Liz just shrugged and took out her phone turning on its flashlight.

"What are you doing?"

"Making a star," Liz said as she pointed the light to the ceiling.

"Seriously?"

"Ready?"

"Okay, ready." They counted down from three and both women broke into a muted version of Starlight Starbright . . ." Then silence. What kind of friend was she, Jeri wondered, debating whether to wish for a good diagnosis for Liz, or a publisher for herself.

"Done?" said Liz.

"Done. . . And don't worry, I wished for you."

"You damn well better have," Liz said.

And Jeri smiled. It was a small lie. Since when do wishes come true?

Gigi and Me—A True Story

The bird lay on the plate.

The violinist wept.

And I screamed "How could you?"

Gigi crossed himself each time we drove past the cemetery where his father lay buried. We could drive up the road, change our minds as to where we were headed, turn around and drive right back and still he'd make the sign of the cross. "Every time?" I'd ask. "Every time!" Gigi would boom back. There was nothing subtle about Gigi. His build: broad. His voice: big. His love of life: almost stereotypically operatic. I felt safe with him. Protected. From the very first time I saw him as I lay flat on my back in a pensione in Pietrasanta, Italy.

At the age of 29, I had realized the time had come for me to decide whether to continue my upward trajectory at an ad agency by day while spending my nights and weekends creating sculpture—or to jump into the abyss and sculpt fulltime earning my keep at whatever odd jobs I could find. Having heard about Pietrasanta from my teacher, the sculptor Bruno Luchessi, I got it in my head that Pietrasanta would be the place where I could not only test out the life of an artist and come to a decision, but cast a number of pieces I had ready to go as well. (At the time—even with the shipping fees—bronze casting cost far less in Italy than New York.) I first checked with the agency as to whether I could take a two month leave of absence—I could. Then I tried out the idea on Bruno. "Perché no?" he said. "You should go. Would be good for you. Call Gigi! He runs the foundry." "You call for me," I said, only to get back, "He speaks enough English, you call!" (This was way before emails, cell phones, even faxes.)

"Certo! Vieni qui!" Gigi told me adding, "I book for you a room at the pensione." Under the assumption that Bruno would be nearby to help me maneuver my way around, I signed up for a crash course in Italian, turned over the reins of my department to the next in line, and most important, managed to find a couple who would live in my apartment rent free in exchange for taking care of my beloved cat, Socrates. This was no easy feat as Socrates had a penchant for eating clothes. Anything not left in a closed drawer or closet was fair game. But I doted on Soc and would never have left New York if I couldn't have arranged for him to stay in his home with a human companion. Although I knew that summer were Bruno's time to be with his family at Marina de Pietrasanta—far away from the town and acolytes like me—upon arriving in Pietrasanta I still reached out to him in desperation crying that I couldn't walk or move. Again he told me to "Call Gigi!"

"You need pasta e brodo!" Gigi declared as he stood at the foot of my bed. When, after a few days, Gigi's Italian version of chicken soup didn't produce a cure, he brought in a doctor. My three weeks at Berlitz had not covered how to ask him what was in the large hypodermic needle he was readying to jam into my thigh. Not that I gave a damn. He had carte blanche so long as it stopped the pain. Incredibly, within hours I was up and walking—a shot of steroids will do that to an inflamed sciatic nerve. It was July 1969 and the start of my summer with Gigi—as well it could be called.

The Tuscany town of Pietrasanta had yet to be invaded by American artists, a situation that would change by the following year. But from the time I arrived until shortly before I left, I was the L'Americana, a scultricci, and an ebrea—a Jew. (I have yet to understand why sculptors, even in English, are too often defined by gender. Why sculptress is acceptable (which it is not to me) but one never hears paint-ress. But I digress. I was open to whatever title they wished to bestow on me as long as it wasn't a donna di vita or di notte. Even though the sexual revolution had begun (and I was more than a willing participant,) I had promised myself I would stay out of all men's beds while abroad. I had a potentially life changing decision to make and I had no doubt that getting it all twisted up in 'he loves me he loves me not' would only confuse the issue. Which brings me back to Gigi. As attractive as he was with those great big dark eyes, thankfully, he was not my type! My taste ran to darker, more complex, difficult men. Besides, he had a wife and I'd sworn off married men.

As I look back on that summer, I have few memories that do not include Gigi. Yes, I took side trips to see more of Italy by myself. And yes, I spent time with Jacques Lipschitz the sculptor who had the studio next to mine. But, here too, Gigi is included as he often took us both to lunch. I remember those conversations to be a blend of English, Italian, French and Spanish filled in with hand gestures for punctuation. Perhaps Gigi and my private talks lacked verbal complexity—we both wanting to learn the other's language—but we delighted in each other's company. In just a few short weeks, I had made a friend that I believed I could count on. One who listened as I tried to explain how conflicted I was. On one hand a strong almost compulsive drive to make sculpture my life's work while simultaneously convinced I wasn't talented enough to do so. As I laid bare my insecurities that often overwhelmed, he did not judge me, but worked to eradicate them. Not by placing a soothing hand on my back, but by leading me into a studio filled with plaster casts of body parts and giving me a supply of drawing materials: paper, charcoal, pencils and ordering me to, "Cominci!" I was to study drawing the way the masters had. And it was in that very same studio, on a Saturday morning six weeks after my arrival, that Gigi found me, dissolved in tears, a letter in my hands from my darling Socrates's caretakers.

"Che è morto?" Gigi asked after taking one look at me. "Who died?"

"It's my cat," I sobbed. "I don't know what to do."

"What you can do if he's dead?"

"He's not dead," I blubbered waving the letter. "He ate their clothes, and they want me to come home or they'll take him to the ASPCA where he'll be put to death."

"So? The cat dies!"

Clearly there was more than a language barrier between us. His English was perfectly clear. An animal is an animal. You hunted with them, petted them, left them outside to fend for themselves, but a member of the family? A stupid Americana idea! "Pazza!" Crazy!

Distraught at the thought of having to leave Italy before I had planned—I'd been toying with the idea of staying even longer—and horrified at the thought of putting a healthy animal to death, I railed at Gigi. He yelled back. Anyone who would have heard us would have thought we were in the midst of a lovers' quarrel. It was he who broke first. "Basta!" he yelled in Italian. "Calma te!" As I sniveled, he told me that I had time to figure out what to do and, in the meantime, he would get a group of friends together for a wonderful evening of bocce and food. "Up the mountain," he said. "The best Florentine chicken in all of

Italy." It would lift my spirits. "Bene?" he asked. "Bene," I replied.

Around five in the afternoon Gigi came by in a station wagon. He'd already gathered up his brother, the Professore di Pintura at the University of Rome; the professor's protégé who had been described to me as a figlio di papa—translation: spoiled brat; along with two men I didn't know one in his eighties. It was difficult enough for me to follow a conversation when it was one-on-one, but with a few people talking at once it was daunting. Still I knew enough words to figure out the gist of what was being said and by carefully watching the behavior of those involved from my perch in the back of the car the scene was anything but pretty. The spoiled brat started viscously teasing the old man by calling him a frocio—the Italian equivalent of faggot. The old man now in tears, demanded he be let out of the car, but Gigi kept driving. At some point Gigi slammed on the brakes, the old man climbed out, and we drove on. I was appalled. Infuriated by the cruelty of it all, and the irreverence shown to an elder by a brat. I yelled at Gigi to turn around and drive the old man back to the village, but he refused saying he would do so once we got to our destination. Besides, Gigi said, the old man had been a Nazi collaborator during the war, he deserved to be treated badly. It made no sense to me. If he was so bad to begin with, why was he invited? Eventually Gigi dropped us off and drove back to find the old man and take him home.

It still amazes me how word of the evening spread. It was as if smoke signals had been set up in Tuscany letting this incredible array of the visiting elite know of the event. (Remember no texting, no Facebook, nor evites.) In addition to us, the guest list consisted of Gigi's other brother, the Professore di Scultore at the University in Florence; the head of Psychologia at the University of Bologna; the Poet Laureate of Italy who as it turned out was slated to be a visiting professor at Smith College in the Fall and the father of a writer who would coincidentally become my neighbor and friend; the writer Luigi Testaferrate who would win the Premio Campiello Prize in 1980 for his book: L'Altissimo e le rose that would include his own description of the evening. (In it I am described as 'la scultrici di New York' who looked like a drawing by Pontorno. He also wrote that I had thick thighs, but I'm told it means something else in Italian— what that is I have never been able to find out.) The last member of our party was the head violinist of the Philharmonic Orchestra of Lucca—a small man with the most beautiful and kindest eyes I'd ever seen. After I'd been introduced to him, almost everyone took me aside to make certain I understood how special he was as he had defied every convention by marrying a single mom with two children from another man.

The violinist and his family lived even higher up in the hills from where we were and I watched and listened as he recounted how earlier in the day he had ridden his motocicletta all the way down the mountain to Viareggio and bought back with him a special bird with which to train his dog to hunt. He seemed to have fallen in love with the bird describing how carefully he had placed it on his motorbike in a cage. Whatever of his story I couldn't catch, Gigi translated for me. I felt as if I was in an Italian movie what with the men playing bocce and others setting up a long table while stringing lights for this special dinner to be served under the stars. "The best Florentine chicken!" Gigi repeated. "The best!" The incident with the old man set aside for another day, the entire scene only reinforced how much I didn't want to leave this country and its people.

Night began to fall and still there was no food. I was starving. My stomach had yet to adapt to the Italian timetable of a shot of espresso in the morning (often with liquor added,) nothing until lunch, and dinner late. But it was now around 8 o'clock and no one had made a move towards the table. Finally, we were called, and everyone took their seats. Did I mention I was the only woman invited? I sat across from Gigi, the professor of psychology to my right and another guest to my left. Two seats further down sat the violinist. "Attencione!" Gigi cried as his brothers brought out a covered platter and headed towards the violinist. "Per te," they said with a grand gesture removing the lid and placing the platter in front of the violinist. "Per te!" they repeated. I could see the violinist's face contort; his eyes well up in agony. "What just happened," I asked Gigi who was now laughing almost uncontrollably. "We cooked the bird!" he said, his laughter slicing through me in all its cruelty.

"How could you, how could you?" I screamed. "How?"

And my good friend, Gigi? The man whom I had trusted to my core. What did he say?

"You don't like killing birds? Then we'll talk about cats!"

I couldn't look at him. The professor tried to calm me. "They're boys, children, who have never grown up. Pay no mind," he said. But I did mind. Horribly. I don't remember eating the chicken when it did finally arrive. I do remember not being able to look at Gigi for the rest of the evening.

The next day I called Bruno. He'd already heard the story. Who called him I have no idea. "It was a joke!" he said.

"It was cruel!" I raged. "The violinist actually cried."

I wanted a show of empathy. All I got was a silent shrug.

———————————

"Mi dispiaci, Senorina," Mario says as he mixes another bucket of plaster. He has come from the foundry in Pietrasanta to make his fortune in New York. "I thought you know."

"When? When did he die?" the plaster covered burlap I hold in my hand suspended. My arms unable to move.

"Il y a seis mesi. No one told you?"

I slam the material into the mold. "She killed him! Always wanting him to take her out dancing. Too much."

Mario grabs my hand. "Calma te!"

"Scusi," I mumble.

"I didn't think you knew her."

"Of course, I knew her. Not well. But I'd met her. Not that she ever invited me to their home."

"I meant the woman who took your place." His eyes stay on the mold, his hand working quickly lest the plaster dry up.

"What place?" I demand. "What are you talking about?"

"You know your place. In his bed after you left. Another Americana scultricci."

I don't know where to place my anger. At the fact Gigi is gone. At Mario and his idiocy. "Gigi and I weren't lovers, Mario. We never even held hands. Nothing. Niente. Just friends."

"Everyone thought. . . then who?"

"Who what?"

"Who you with?"

"No one for God's sake." I can see he doesn't believe me. The male species, 'if you're not with me, you must be with someone else.' I let it go. I have a piece to cast. We finish the mold and I leave. I don't shed one tear. Not one. who so easily cry.

Addendum

I never saw Socrates again. My neighbor, whose children had taken my apartment for the summer, brought Soc to his factory where he turned out to be an incredible mouser. My neighbor asked if I wanted to see him and I said no. I needed a time out from animals and was fearful if I saw him, I'd take him back. Once Soc rid the factory of mice, one of the workers there took him to a farm in upstate New York. I have no reason to doubt the story. My neighbor was an honorable man.

A year later I adopted Pablo. A year after that Miquel. When he died Mischa entered the picture, then Bouche, Kirlegirl and lastly, Benjison. For forty years I made it up to Soc. No cat was ever left alone overnight. They were fed almost always on time. And except for a period of mourning when one died, they had a companion. They were simply the best friends anyone could have.

After Thirty Years?

From: Sframton6@aol.com

To: Lori@BrandonArt.com

Subject: After thirty years . . . Really?

Dear Lori:

I have apologized once and will apologize again though I truly don't understand why you're so aggrieved. You told us that if we didn't take the triptych, it would most likely end up on the street. I thought it extremely generous of Paul to offer to house it. Besides, we assumed the panels were a gift and as we had no one to whom we could regift them, what were we to do? I think you should be grateful that they hung on our wall for the ten years they did. I told you we were planning on renovating and I am sorry we couldn't build our home around your work. (A 9'8" triptych takes up a lot of wall space.) If you hadn't asked where we'd hung it, you wouldn't have known we threw it out. It's not as if you visit. When was the last time? Nine years ago? And then I am certain it was only to see your piece on somebody else's wall.

By the way, you were the one who told me to get over my mother giving away my Barbie Doll Collection and I did.

Perhaps you should take your own advice and do the same.

Susan

From: Lori@BrandonArt.com
To: Sframton6@aol.com

Subject: After thirty years . . . Yes really!

Dear Susan:

Do you really consider that an email comparing an artist's work to a collection of Barbie dolls an apology? And yes, I said I was desperate to find homes for "my work," and I probably said I feared some of it might end up out on the street, but I never said that if "you" didn't take that particular piece, that's where it would land. I said if "someone" didn't. If you recall, I had a few more weeks before I was to be evicted—still time to find it a permanent home. (Please notice the underline under permanent.)

To be clear, it was Paul who professed his desire to have it and I distinctly remember questioning him as to whether he was certain. I was quite aware that a large work rendered in shades of white, grey and black could be difficult to live with. Thinking of it lying on top of a landfill with a crow attempting to pluck out Eve's eyes is more than a little painful. At least your mother had the decency to give your dolls to another child to enjoy!

Lori

From: Sframton6@aol.com

To: Lori@BrandonArt.com

Subject: After thirty years . . . Shame on you!

My dear Lori:

I should have learned by now that self-absorption is the hallmark of the artist personality. You know all too well my Barbies and the loss of them epitomized the extremely conflicted relationship I had with my mother (may she finally rest in peace.) I think it's downright hypocritical of you to take exception to the comparison. Wasn't it you who said it should have been my decision as to whom and where my dolls went, if they should have gone at all? Not to mention how much they would be worth today. I am quite certain your art has not appreciated in value half as much as they have.

Susan

From: Lori@BrandonArt.com

To: Sframton6@aol.com

Subject: After thirty years. . . Shame on me?

Susan!

How the hell would you know what my art is selling for? You sat at lunch going into every detail of your renovation. While you babbled on I played a game with myself as to when and if you would inquire as to my well-being and only when you finally took a bite of the blackened tuna on the bed of Goma Wakame which I made myself, schlepping to an Asian market across town in order to get the right ingredients, did I get an opening to ask where you'd hung the piece. I was so stunned by your "We threw it out" (a direct quote) that all I could think of was how to get the meal over and done with so I could get you the hell out of my home. (By the way you didn't even acknowledge what it took to come up with a meal free of gluten, lactose, eggs, nuts and whatever else was on your goddamn list. I might be an artist, but I'm not a sorcerer.)

Lori

And oh! I had made a dessert—just decided not to serve it.

From: Sframton6@aol.com

To: Lori@BrandonArt.com

Subject: After thirty years . . . Yes, you!

Lori:

For your information, I kept talking to avoid having to eat what you served. I hate HATE raw fish. The only reason I hadn't added it to my list of what I cannot consume—something I always do out of consideration for my host—was that I knew what a tight budget you live on. It never dawned on me you would splurge on tuna. It took all my strength to take that first bite. I wanted to throw up. So, when you asked about what we did with your work, out came the past tense of "throw" instead of something more benign.

And, as long as I'm being totally honest, I never liked the piece to begin with and didn't know what to do when Paul said he'd take it, so I bit my tongue. At that point in time we were discussing marriage and I didn't want to put a wedge between us. As it is, your piece has caused considerable consternation. You and your sexual imaging.

Susan

By the way, you can order Japanese seaweed on-line at Amazon.

From: Lori@BrandonArt.com

To: Sframton6@aol.com

Subject: After thirty years . . . You're kidding?

Susan! You entered into a marriage in which you weren't comfortable sharing your opinion? What were all those years of group therapy about? All those sessions during which we had to point out how manipulative you were being by professing you were too frightened to express yourself so we would focus on you. Well clearly, you've come a long way since you're letting me know you never liked the piece. That's as direct as it comes. Makes me wonder if you ever liked any of my work.

And just so you know, you are not being considerate by giving a host a list of what you can and cannot eat. Nor did you have to make such a huge thing about climbing four flights of stairs arriving as if you'd taken your last breath. Perhaps you should consider going to a gym.

L-

P.S. I was taught that when you're a guest, you eat what the host prepares. And if you're so afraid you'll starve, bring your own bloody sandwich.

From: Sframton6@aol.com

To: Lori@BrandonArt.com

Subject: After thirty years . . . Clearly, we were brought up differently.

I was taught that it was rude to leave food on your plate when someone has gone to the trouble to cook for you. (And I do go to a gym. Twice a week.)

As to my not liking your work. Please! Now who's being manipulative? You always needed the group to tell you how good you were. And we all did. We supported you through session after session, rant after rant about the art world and how cruel it was—listening ad nauseum to your crying poverty and exhaustion. As to our "tossing" your work. You threw out plenty during your so-called artistic slumps. At least that's what you told the group. If you didn't value your work, why should we have to? S-

By the way, if you were so poor, how could you afford therapy?

From: Lori@BrandonArt.com

To: Sframton6@aol.com

Subject: After thirty years . . . She had a sliding scale.

Oh, for heaven's sake. All serious artists destroy work that is not coming to fruition or that doesn't coalesce. We only keep work we believe worthy of a life. And that triptych was that and much more. I'm glad that my work caused problems in your marriage—it means it was controversial and probing. Though how an abstraction can render destruction to a supposedly solid relationship is beyond me. Abstract paintings are like Rorschach test—it's what the viewer sees not what the artist intends. What did you imagine you saw? Did you cover what disturbed you with fig leaves? You always were a puritan at heart.

From: Sframton6@aol.com

To: Lori@BrandonArt.com

Subject: After thirty years . . . You don't have to be snide.

The title alone was a sexual road map. Besides, it was not what I saw, it's what Paul did. Said Adam's gyrations were an inspiration. He wanted it hung across from our bed. My bedroom was pale pink with touches of mint and fuchsia and I'd be damned if I'd let it ruin my décor. Not to mention my sleep. And it would have. Paul being sexually inventive requires me to turn into a Cirque de Soleil contortionist. And while I understand the importance of keeping sex alive in a marriage, having to limber up before going to bed after downing half a bottle of wine is not my idea of fun. But then you would have no idea of what it takes to keep a marriage going—your idea of a relationship is a quickie in a plane bathroom. So, don't question me on what damage an abstract painting can cause.

From: Lori@BrandonArt.com

To: Sframton6@aol.com

Subject: After thirty years . . . talk about being snide.

If you want to start pulling up personal divulges offered up in the sanctity of a group therapy session, please feel free. And I will feel free to include Paul in my next email. I wonder if he would be interested in knowing that your desire to be married superseded your desire for any particular man.

From: Sframton6@aol.com

To: Lori@BrandonArt.com

Subject: After thirty years . . .Enough!

I think we have said all we need to. Your insatiable desire to wreak vengeance upon an innocent act of what we considered a kindness—sparing you the pain of knowing we could no longer keep the piece—means you haven't changed one iota from the days when you fantasized about annihilating various gallery owners. Obviously, you only got out of therapy what you paid for—which according to you was next to nothing. Too bad.

From: Lori@BrandonArt.com

To: Sframton6@aol.com

Subject: After thirty years . . . Enough is right!

And you, my dear Susan, obviously still cannot get past your-self. I was the one who supported your claim that your mother should have asked you what to do with your beloved Barbies. Did it even once dawn on you to pick up the phone and give me the same consideration? If you had, I would have told you what

I had planned to tell you at lunch. That I have been taken on by a major gallery! My first one-woman show is set for the fall. If your announcement hadn't sickened me to the core, I would also have told you that upon seeing the photos of the piece I had trusted you to preserve, the gallery owner had wanted to include it in the show. It's size alone would have made it one of the major works shown. As it no longer exists, what I've decided to do is to create a framed montage from the photos of the piece and hang it in the show. I will title it: Adam and Eve Descending into Hell destroyed by Susan Framton. Like mother like daughter.

The North and the South of It

—We don't have to do this, he said. But for some ungodly reason, I told him I was fine. So, there I was with a total stranger, in a red, top down, sporty convertible on an unlit back road outside Asheville, wondering if I was going to live to tell the tale. All because I had promised Betts, I'd show her how to pick up a man for a one-night stand. But then, in those days, I was a teacher. Taught kids at a private school how to draw, paint, model clay. (That saying about those who can do and those who can't teach? Well, it's crap. How about those of us who do need to put food in our mouths?) Back then private schools didn't require a teaching degree, so I was able to secure a job. It was also why they could get away with paying me next to nothing. In other words, after shelling out money for rent, food, and my own art supplies, there wasn't much left for a real vacation. Which is why for the past three years I'd gone down to Betts over the Easter break.

After college when she moved South to live with her parents who had relocated, and I had returned to New York, we were on the phone constantly as if we were still roomies. Our conversations didn't stop even after she married Jim (I was her maid of honor) and she'd come up to New York to shop, then head to my place where we'd sit and talk into the night. The times that

Jim came along I'd only get to see her at dinner before they took in a show. He was all over her in those days, seeming to refute my Dad's, "If they make a big display in public, nothing's going on at home." And she certainly radiated satisfaction.

Our lives moved in vastly different directions after Jim, Jr. was born, as did what we cared about. For her it was all about "her boys," her new women friends from the club, and what she served to whom when she entertained. I was mired in how to make ends meet, finding the time and energy to come home after a full day of teaching and produce art, and maybe, just maybe get laid. There came a point when our past no longer bound us and the present split us apart. In the space of a few years we'd gone from best friends who confided every thought we had, to phone calls on or around our birthdays, along with the obligatory Christmas card. Mine were in whatever medium I was playing with that year: gouache; litho; montage. Betts's were a photographic chronicle of her existence from one year to the next: she and Jim cozied up in the nursery with Jim Jr.; followed by all three with their dog in front of a house; then another dog and a newer house—along with an imprinted message. I did take note how rigid her smile had become, but figured, that unlike me, she was exhausted from holiday demands.

As my fortieth birthday loomed, I began to take stock of my life. It wasn't pretty. I hadn't secured a gallery, nor a major commission, nor had I been able to move out of the rundown loft I lived in. And of course, I couldn't help but compare myself to what I imagined Betts's life to be like. She must have been doing the same because a few days before hers, she phoned. —Doing decade-al accounting? I asked. And she said, —Why Laura sweetie, that's just what I was doing. And I was thinking we should celebrate our fortieth together, don't you? Back in college she talked like the rest of us from New York, but it seemed that over the years, she'd turned into Miss Scarlet herself, complete with drawl and lilt. —You've never tasted southern hospitality, now have you?

I figured that years of living in Asheville had gotten to her. Either that or she felt she had to out southern the southerners to be accepted. —Now I'm not going to take no for an answer, she said. Why you just get yourself down here so we can celebrate together. I didn't mention that my birthday had passed and at first, I declined. The idea of visiting someone who seemed to have morphed into an alien creature and now lived in the perfect house, had the perfect marriage, the perfect kid–not to mention those dogs–seemed way too masochistic even for me. Persistence was probably one of the only traits we shared and this steel magnolia kept at it, calling regularly until eventually the allure of mint juleps, or at least a better scotch than I could afford, along with imagined plush comfortable chairs to sink into, warmer weather, and a few days off from having to fend for myself, won out. I set aside my qualms that envy might send me spiraling down deeper into the depression I was already heading towards and told her she had me for better or worse.

On that first flight down, I found myself seated next to an attractive, ring-less man—somewhere around my age—with smiley eyes that spelled seduction. I can't remember which of us initiated the conversation, but once we started, we didn't stop. We talked about politics, careers, what it was like to live in New York, what it was like to live in Asheville. I kept trying to figure out if there was a wife and kids in the picture, but he didn't allude to any, so I allowed my mind to race ahead full speed. Would he consider moving to New York if he and I went the whole nine yards? Could I live in the South? I was at the point of considering dual commuting when the plane landed.

We left the plane together. A smashing couple if I do say so. And there was Betts waving at me, as well as a woman whom I assumed to be a friend of hers, a real plain-Jane, waving as well. I waved back. Then I saw he too was waving—at the plain-Jane. I managed to keep smiling. Wife-y did the same. We met up, introduced ourselves, and it took no more than a minute, before plain-Jane whisked him away in one direction, and Betts and I went off in another.

We were a study in contrasts, Betts and me. She in a spotless white, buttoned down, ironed cotton blouse, a blue and green tartan plaid pleated skirt that came just above her knees, a blue matching cardigan and white sneakers. I wore my usual flowered cotton pants, tie dye tunic, sandals and long dangly earrings. As we headed towards the car, Betts couldn't contain herself. —My Lord, Laura. How did you manage to snag the best-looking man on board? —Didn't snag, I said. —Got seated next to. Not that it made any difference, he's taken. Which is a shame as I haven't had sex in months. And what did Betts say? The woman whom I would have sworn was getting it regularly. The woman who had the marriage made in heaven. —Well lucky you, she said. —It's been five years for me!

I was so stunned I found it difficult to keep walking. —I can't tell you how relieved I am to have you here, Laura, she said. —I've had no one to speak with about any of this. By now we were at the car putting my one straw bag with two changes of clothes and another with the gifts I'd brought in the trunk. —What about your friends from the club? I asked, the scene I had walked into sinking in. —For heaven's sake, Laura. They may be friends, but they're not confidantes. Whatever I'd tell them could get back to Jim and that would be the end for me. Besides, the women down here avoid any discussion of marital discord that could lead to divorce—too frightening.

So much for my free R&R. As my Dad used to say—he had a lot of sayings—'Everything has its price.' Whatever small pangs of guilt I felt about only bringing a book of phantasmagoria for Jim Jr. and two dozen New York bagels for Betts, vanished. It was clear that my room and board was going to be paid for by my being a receptacle for five years of bottled up pain. —You have no idea what it's like down here, Laura, Betts went on. —All the lawyers belong to the same club. Literally and figuratively. It's perfectly fine for them to fight each other down to the last golf ball for a client, as long as the client isn't one of their wives. Then it's as if they're all at the same firm. Between Jim and his connections, I could lose everything, including Jim Jr.

As we drove to her home, I couldn't decide whether Jim had turned off because she'd turned into a Stepford Wife or she'd become a Stepford Wife because of Jim turning off. The question was put to rest that evening. We were having drinks in their den. A wood paneled room dedicated to cocktails with a long flip top bar counter, a mirror shelved wall stocked with liquor and glasses, and of course bar stools. I loved it. Not that the rest of the house wasn't right out of House Beautiful southern style, but what with the volume of needle point pillows on every chair, polished silver candlesticks and bowls, every bit of space taken up with some object or another, this was the only room that came close to feeling familiar. Betts had gone to the kitchen to get dinner ready with a truly southern —Now you just stay where you are, Laura. You're supposed to be on vacation. And I was more than happy to do so until I felt a grab ass hand on me. It wasn't the first time a friend's husband had pulled that stunt. Men see an unattached female and assume she's either a nympho who can't say no even if she wants to, or gay and just need the right man to turn her straight. I was neither and slapped his hand away, but that didn't wipe the 'I know you want it' leer off his face. Even with what Betts had told me about their loveless marriage, I wasn't sure if I should let her know what had transpired. I decided to keep my mouth shut.

The next morning Betts and I were in our robes. Mine, one of her guest terries and hers, a boudoir white silk with lace, when Jim entered all suited up for the office. Real pinstriped attorney style. He put down his briefcase, wrapped his arms around her waist, picking her up so that her feet dangled. His eyes on me the whole time. I watched him squeeze until her back cracked and she let out an —Oh, Jim! which could have meant anything from 'Thanks, I needed that' to 'Cut the crap!' It was hard to tell. After he left, I asked if he did that often and she said —That's what goes for sex nowadays. Better than nothing.

Listening to Betts go on about the facade of her marriage, the lack of any real communication amongst friends, I couldn't imagine how we'd reconnect. While she'd been stuck in a 50's movie, I'd marched against the war, smoked pot, picked up men at bars, and went to meetings about women's sexuality where we stared at our vulvas and taught ourselves the art of the dildo. How we were going to find common ground eluded me.

Thankfully, Jim Sr. decided to take Jim Jr., camping and slowly the old Betts began to emerge. Not all of her, but enough so she was recognizable despite her white sneakers that stayed white the entire time I was there. Now, don't get me wrong, it wasn't all one-sided. Betts did ask questions about my life. What it was like to go it alone. To be only responsible for oneself. Sometimes she'd question me about my various affairs. And I obliged with as much information as I could without getting too graphic. Even I had my limits. And while the picture I painted wasn't always appealing, at least I had the possibility of better things ahead by not being shackled to a bastard. By the end of that first visit, Betts decided she'd had enough as far as Jim Sr. was concerned. The proverbial last straw the pass he made at me. Yes, I'd told her.

It took a few months, but eventually she found a lawyer up in Raleigh. A female. One who'd been so screwed by her first husband that she'd returned to school and got her law degree just so she could reap revenge by proxy. If her clients' husbands were lawyers, as hers had been, so much the better. When the news got out about Betts upcoming divorce, she began to hear stories about Jim's groping hands; the women he'd pawed out in the open; the secretary he'd been screwing forever. I never asked her what it was like to have spent years creating the perfect home only to find out that everyone knew it to be a lie. The shame alone had to be sickening.

By the time I returned the following Easter, Betts and Jim were still battling over the fine print. Betts's lawyer hadn't let her move out, and Jim knew enough to stay put so as not to lose his claim on the property. I pitied their kid. He had to negotiate his way between the two of them on a daily basis. Not that I ever saw the younger Jim more than one night a year, the Easter camping trip now a ritual. Still, it only took a quick glance at his drawn face and wary eyes, to know some shrink was going to have a field day down the road.

Around February of the next year, they'd reached a settlement. Jim Sr. would officially move out so there would be no break in Jim Jr.'s living arrangements. Then, after seven years when Jim Jr. was ready for college, Betts would be expected to be self-supporting and Jim Sr. would buy her share of the house. (Not that he wanted to live there; he just didn't want her to.) By March his clothes were gone, along with some of the furniture and he'd rented a place within walking distance so that Jim Jr. could visit. In April, I arrived with two bottles of champagne— one for each of us though I had nothing to celebrate.

After Betts bundled Jim Jr. off to Jim Sr.'s, she and I got into our robe—warm flannel affairs—curled up in her cushioned chairs in the den and cracked open the first bottle. We didn't need a catch-up. By now we'd been on the phone at least once a week. I was getting pleasantly soused when I became aware of a car slowly driving back and forth in front of the house. I looked quizzically at Betts. —It's Jim, she said. —He drives by every night to remind me that I'm a boarder and I'd better not damage his property. When I asked if she had any more thoughts on what she was going to do to earn money, she told me she still didn't know. —The only job I had was at that publishing house, remember? Which was more a flunky than anything else. I could go back to school and get a Masters in something. Jim would have to pay. My lawyer made sure to put that in our agreement. I don't know, Laura. I'm still trying to figure it out.

She sounded beaten and I started to get 'the guilts.' Not that I had talked her into leaving Jim. If she hadn't wanted to, she'd never have invited me in the first place. Of all the people in her life, she subliminally knew I'd be the one to urge her to go it alone. —Listen, I said. —How about we get out of here tomorrow night? Go to a bar or something. We might even meet some men. —Oh, I don't know, she said. When I asked why not as her was divorce final, she just shrugged. —By my count, I said, —you haven't been to bed with a man for at least eight years. Don't you think it's about time? —I wouldn't know how, she said. And I countered with, —For Christ's sake. It's like riding a bike and she said, —I didn't mean how to have sex. Just how to pick someone up. Never ever did it, she said.

Finally, I could be of use! I could show her how to get laid. I convinced her to give it a try and we spent the rest of the evening figuring out which restaurant in the area had a bar that catered to singles and found two. The next day we drove by each to see which one looked more appealing. With their painted white fronts, blue awnings, parking lots in the rear, I couldn't tell the difference, but Betts could. —This one will get a better crowd, she said. —The cars tell all. I told her to pick whichever one made her comfortable and we spent the rest of the day dolling ourselves up. I even put on makeup. Then, at 7:30 sharp, we went off in search of prey.

I quickly realized I was in alien territory. In New York in those days, you knew someone's occupation by the bar they chose. The White Horse got mostly writers and actors. Fanelli's the artists, especially those who had to teach to supplement their incomes, in other words my hangout. The Cedar Tavern, mostly tourists and art students who thought they could improve their output by rubbing up against the walls where Pollack and de Kooning once held court. Max's Kansas City got the more swinging crowd of photographers, models, and the current hot art world names. Even if you hit a night where no one went where they were expected to go, you still could get a feel as to who was who by their appearance. The painters always had some paint splattered on them somewhere; the sculptors proudly displayed their cuts, bruises and burn marks of the day, and the photographers lived in black pants, black shirts, black shoes and either shaved their heads or sported ponytails. In those days, the male artists outnumbered us females twenty to one. Still I had to compete against art students or would-be artist's wives for a man's attention. And sure, I could mistake a fragile looking conceptual artist—the kind who built landscapes out of sand and sticks—for a writer, but by and large I my instincts were right on. (There was the night of the plumber, but he'd hung around the art scene for so long, who could tell?) Anyway, in Asheville, I was totally out of my element. These guys could have worked for the phone company stringing lines, bagged groceries, or sat at a desk. With no markers to go by, I imagined them all spending their weekends shooting guns, racing cars or roping cattle, although I assumed we were way too far east for that.

We'd been at the bar for about fifteen minutes when I noticed a guy perched on a stool down at the far end. It was hard to tell his height, but he looked relatively cute, light brown hair, good build. I told Betts to watch and smiled at him. Not a full smile—just a subtle tease. He nodded back with an imperceptible movement of the head. I turned back to Betts. —That's the opener, I said. —Really? That's it? —That's it. Act One Scene One.

Intent on continuing my lesson, I tilted my head towards him again and then back towards us, suggesting he come over, which, of course, he did. So far, not so different from New York and just before he slid into the stool next to me, I whispered to Betts, —In for a penny. . .

From there it was easy. A little conversation, followed by a foot, mine, resting on his shoe. I figured I would tell Betts about the foot thing later. After a while Betts got the message that he and I were into each other. Which, for the moment, I was. So, she excused herself. Said she was tired. —Now you stay as long as you want, Laura, you hear? And you, sir, you bring her home safe and sound. The southern belle was back.

Which is how I found myself driving to God knows where in the middle of the night—well really more like 10PM—with a total stranger. For the first half of the ride, we didn't say much of anything. Then I confessed. Told him that it had all been a show for my friend. That's when he asked if I wanted to turn back, and even though I wanted to say yes, I couldn't bring myself to do so. Sort of like that old joke about losing your virginity because you didn't want to appear rude. Besides, part of me was curious. Not about him. But about whether I would make it out alive. I'm serious. My life had been so drab of late that the thought of tempting fate appealed. Ten years of teaching kids who could care less. Rejection after rejection at galleries. The longest relationship I'd managed to sustain was probably just over three weeks, the exceptions being one or two European artists whom I'd see whenever they came to town. Meanwhile most of my friends seemed to be moving on with their lives. Even Betts had made a change. It's not that I wanted to get killed or anything like that. Nor was I making some crazy pact with God. You know, Oh Lord, get me out of this alive and I promise to change my ways. Nothing like that. Just that part of me thought that by courting danger, I could shake things up a bit.

Eventually we arrived at what appeared to be a one-level shack plopped down in the middle of a wooded area. The southern kind. Trees that looked like they were a cross between a huge oak and a palm. Not that I could see much. It was pitch black.

He left the car lights on and got out, not coming come around to my side and opening the car door or anything like that. Just got out and expected I'd follow. I imagined I'd find a bed, cans of beer on the floor, and a lantern. Where the lantern idea came from, I'm not sure, except that I figured no one bothered to string electrical wires this far out. He walked onto the porch, unlocked the door, flicked on an actual light switch, and stood there waiting for me to enter. Well you wouldn't have believed it. I certainly didn't. There along the walls hung two Mondrians, one Matisse, and a Kline. Not originals, obviously, still. How the hell did he know from Kline?

—Not bad for a redneck, huh? he said reading my face. He must have been waiting for that moment the whole ride out. I forced my eyes away from the wall and looked around. The place was similar to mine back home, only smaller. One open room with a fridge, stove, and counter along one wall. A round table in the middle. A few chairs. Small sofa. A bed, double. And then, lining the back wall, windows. His furniture wasn't half bad either. Leather, black, with some red pillows. Could have come right out of a magazine. It crossed my mind that maybe some woman had done it up for him or that he'd been married, and this was what his ex no longer wanted. He became someone to find out about, but he wasn't interested in conversation. He grabbed a beer, offered me one, which I refused, and headed towards the bed. —It's late, he said, and I answered —Right!

Once we were in bed pulling off our own clothes, he gave me another out. —We don't have to have sex, he said.

In retrospect, he probably felt as uninterested as I was. I wanted to talk. To find out about him, but once again I said, —No, it's okay. We started in like two bad dancers going through the motions. The sex lousy, though he did achieve orgasm. And no, I didn't fake one. Not that he cared. When he was done, he just rolled over after giving me one of those 'there, there' pats on my rear. In New York I'd have gotten up and gone home. Here I had no choice. In for a penny, my eye.

The next morning it was as if I didn't exist. He grabbed a beer out of the fridge, and when I said, 'good morning,' he demanded that I get a move on so he wouldn't be late for work. I can't remember what kind of work he did, or if he even told me. Most likely he did, but it was so removed from my world that it never registered. We drove to Betts's in silence. I kept trying to figure out what I'd say to her. If I was honest about how lousy a night I'd had, she might not ever try it for herself, and that would be a real waste of my energies. I was fantasizing a long shower when he pulled up to the curb, reached across me to open my door, and made a big thing of time passing by drumming his fingers on the wheel. I think I made some dumb remark like, —Well, you know where we are. I got out and walked up the driveway fully expecting Betts to rush out to greet me. Instead there was a note pinned on the front door: L, I'm at Charlotte Memorial, Jim Jr. hurt. Meet me there. B

I'm sure Betts figured that my so-called date would drive me to the hospital, but he was long gone so I ran to a neighbor's who called me a cab, and off I went. I can tell you that for the next few days, until it was clear that Jim Jr. was going to be fine— he'd fallen into a ravine and hit his head—the last thing on either of our minds was my 'teaching moment.' By the time it did come up all I told her about was the art on the redneck's walls. It sufficed. She had no interest in the sex act itself and I had no desire to discuss a failure. Not because she might turn off getting 'out there,' but because I had begun to turn off on myself. Normally I luxuriate in a long shower, but each time I stood with the water spraying over me, I relived his refusal to acknowledge my existence, his wanting me gone and I'd be soaped, rinsed and out in a matter of minutes. I attempted to console myself with the thought that whoever hung those paintings, it sure wasn't someone who reached for a beer at 7 o'clock in the morning.

Betts and I continued to talk every week. I'd report to her on my latest attempts to find a dealer; she, on trying to find work so she could take care of herself once Jim Jr. went off to college and child support, along with alimony, ceased. Whatever suggestions I made she greeted with a negative and I listened as she became more and more demoralized. —Someone even told me to get a job as a saleswoman. I mean, really, Laura! Now, I'm not denigrating sales folk, I'm not. But a sales job is not going to support me, not one tiny bit. I decided to ignore the hint of the southern accent that was creeping back in. I then suggested going to work for a decorator. —It would be perfect for you, I said. —After a while, you could go out on your own. I bet a slew of clients would follow you. Clearly, I had pushed too hard. —Enough! she snapped. —I don't need your help. You've helped enough now, haven't you?

I wondered if she'd begun to blame me for the quandary, she was now in. —I've only tried to be there for you, I said. And she confirmed my suspicions with, —Well you have, haven't you? Pushing me to divorce Jim. Pushing me to go out and lay a stranger. Thank God I didn't do that. Pushing me to find work. Pushing pushing pushing! Her voice verging on hysteria. —Betts, I said as calmly as I could, —You're just scared. It will work out, promise! I could hear her sobbing on the other end of the phone. A few minutes passed and then she offered her apologies. —I'm so sorry, Laura, she said. —I didn't mean any of that. I guess it's all too much for me. And I told her I understood, though I wondered if deep down, she had meant every word.

A few months later Betts called all excited. Friends had arranged for her to meet a man they knew, a business associate. —A blind date, Laura. Can you imagine? Supposedly, he's dated everyone between here and Charlotte. Oh, Laura, I'm a nervous wreck. I don't have your experience. Jim's the only man I've ever been with.

It was the way she said it that rankled. Yes, I was more experienced when it came to men. But her undertone implied something else. I brushed it aside aware it could just be my own reaction to that lousy night. I told her she'd do just fine and called the next day to see how it went. —Fine, her answer. —There's got to be more than just 'fine.' I said and she said, —Well, he's divorced. A realtor. Two kids. They live with the mother. —Is he cute at least? I asked and the matter-of-fact way she said that he was nice looking, told me there was no attraction. —Well, if there's one, there's two, I said, and here again hopelessness crept back into her voice. —Maybe, she said. —Slim pickings around here.

Betts went out with him again. And again. And then again. —So, it's serious, I said. And she answered with the vowels drawn out, —He's very considerate. And there's not a lawyer in his family.

We talked less and less as she and Marlin—that was his name, Marlin— continued to see each other. I asked her once how the sex was and all I got back was an —Oh, Laura. It sounded no different than her old 'Oh, Jim.' She did invite me to come down during the Easter break the following year, but it didn't seem right to go—her being in a new relationship and all. She didn't sound disappointed either when I said I couldn't.

I also didn't make it to the wedding. Can't remember why exactly. Probably too much money for an overnighter what with air fare, hotel, cabs and everything. Or more likely I was feeling sorry for myself. My so-called teaching moment in the outskirts of Asheville had caused me to be a bit more discerning which meant there were fewer partners back home to pick from. Besides, it was one thing to be a maid-of-honor in my twenties and quite another to stand off to the side, and watch a friend remarry as I moved alone into my 50's.

On the rare occasions when we did speak, some of the old superficiality returned. She seamlessly moved back into running a household, having friends from the club for dinner, going with Marlin to business gatherings. There was no mention of a job. Sometimes she'd put Marlin on the phone with me. —Now say hello you two. And he and I would make polite chatter about nothing, neither of us knowing why we were being told to communicate.

I finally secured a gallery and was preparing for a show when Betts called to say she and Marlin were coming up to New York for a visit and would I like to join them for dinner. —I just can't wait for you two to meet, she said. —And just to play it safe, I'm going to make sure I sit between you, her voice so sweet why butter would melt as she might say. —Betts, I had nothing to do with Jim's laying his hand on me and you know that. —Oh, Laura, I was just messing with you. —That's not what it sounded like. And what does she come back with? —Well, your incident certainly was the nail in the coffin, now wasn't it? The sweet butter churning. I began to lose control. —That coffin, Betts, already had a slew of nails hammered in! —Oh, Laura, for heaven's sake, I know that. Now listen, we're leaving it to you to find us a nice restaurant and make a reservation. We're staying at the W, so something close to the hotel. Okay? —Sure, I said, my tone not the warmest. We said our goodbyes and I hung up the phone.

I lost any desire to go. Not that the invitation had enticed to begin with. I'd seen enough pictures of Marlin to know how bland he appeared. But now Betts' recreation of hers and Jim's history had made me the villain. Whether she was just 'messing with me' or not, remarks she'd made over the years began to pop up as I tried to go back to work. Her 'Well just look at you! First of our crowd to lose her virginity! Jim and I've decided to wait until we're married.' Her 'Why you 70's women! You really are something, aren't you? Examining your private parts. I leave that to my gynecologist.' And her, 'Well, I must say, Laura. You certainly showed me how to lay a stranger. Not something I'm going to do any time soon. But thank you, Laura. That was most kind.' How had I not heard what she was actually saying? Missed her profound disapproval? Suddenly I saw myself in her eyes and felt nauseated.

I walked over to a mirror and took note. A wrinkle here and there. Strands of grey that if I wanted, could be touched up. But I liked them. Each one hard-earned as I often boasted. No! I was who I had chosen to be, and I'd be damned if I would permit myself to see me as Betts most likely did. So, I had gone off with a stranger to have sex and it had ended in disgust. We all do stupid things. But it was gutsy and daring. Could Betts say the same about any of her choices? I made the reservation at the Gramercy but when the time came, begged off. Lied and told her I'd been hit with a stomach bug. —We'll miss you terribly, Betts said. —Me you too, I lied back.

Eventually, it was just Christmas cards again until even those stopped. It had been a number of years since we'd been in touch, but a few weeks ago, on a whim, I sent her a brochure of my latest show. That decade-al assessment thing again. Okay, so maybe it was my way to laud it over her. That all on my own, I'd done pretty well. So far, I haven't heard a word back.

Lotte and I
Through a Friendship Darkly

"I might be in New York in two weeks," the voice on the other end of the phone had said. How well I knew that Yugoslavian accent. "Have to chaperone a group to Madrid," she'd added. "And hello to you too, Lotte," I'd quipped. It's one of those friendships that got picked up as if no time has passed, even after a few years, as was once again the case. "What kind of group?" I'd asked. "For my job," her response if it was obvious. I had no idea what she was talking about. But then Lotte's life had always seemed a jigsaw puzzle with most of the pieces missing.

I am in Chicago on business. Have come earlier than needed so that I could spend time with Lotte. It's been ages since we've talked, longer since we've gotten together. Other than her putting on a few pounds and both of us making attempts to hide the grey, I am certain we would have no trouble recognizing each other if we accidently passed on the street. On the flight out from New York, my thoughts had wandered away from my reading, and it came to me that I had no recollection of how we'd become friends, never-the-less how we'd met. I knew it had to be in our late teens or early twenties. I remembered going with her to a party at which she'd introduced me to the off-spring of famous parents—Jane Fonda, Tina Crawford neither famous themselves at the time—but I had no idea as to how she'd gotten us invited or if she'd known them before. Nor could I recall where she'd lived or if I'd ever met her parents. She certainly had known mine. My mother would have said she lived at our house. I went back to my book figuring that at some point in our time together, she could fill me in.

Now, as we amble along Chicago's Riverwalk, Lotte tells me that her husband Michael has had a stroke. She has an off-handed way of speaking, punctuating her sentences by flicking her slender fingers with their long red nails into the air so that his 'stroke' sounds as if he ate a sandwich that disagreed with him. "He won't be like you remember him," she adds.

But I don't remember him. "I'm so sorry, Lotte," I say. "That has to be hard on you."

She nods and recites some of the details. Where he was, who found him, the time in the hospital.

"Remind me when I met him?"

"He took you to dinner. In New York. I arranged it," she says.

And immediately I can see myself in an upscale restaurant sitting across from a much older, heavily built, but attractive man with a European accent in a slightly shiny dark blue suit. I also remember I had a negative reaction to his attempts at charm. Too full of himself. Definitely too old for Lotte. "Did you grow to love him?" I ask. It is a perfectly fair question. Years before she'd told me that she'd had no choice as to whom she could marry. Something to do with her father—a bigwig in Tito's government—money, or the lack thereof, and politics. I never fully understood her explanation. Nor do I think she explained it so that I would. "Did you? Grow to love him?" I repeat.

She doesn't answer. Doesn't break her stride. I leave it alone.

Suddenly Lili pops to mind. We three haven't been together for well over thirty years. The trio! Lotte with her Yugoslavian accent, the epitome of a woman who knew more about sex, men, life! than I ever would. Lili, uninhibited, vibrant, daring, Lili the Greek. I can still see her standing on the edge of the sea lions' enclosure in the Central Park Zoo loudly imitating their sounds and clapping her hands as if they were flippers while I pretend, I don't know her. "Are you still in touch with Lili?" I ask. "There were times I thought she'd get us arrested."

Lotte stops and turns to me. "Lili committed suicide," she says with a wisp of exasperation. "I'm sure I told you."

For a moment, my breath leaves. I can't believe I could have forgotten. "Why?" I ask. "For God's sake, she was so full of life!"

And Lotte explains that Lili hated her marriage, her life. Felt trapped.

I wonder if Lotte is describing herself as well as Lili. We start to walk again. Slowly. In silence. That of the three of us it would be Lili to end up taking her own life, seems unimaginable. If anyone, I think, it could have been me. In those years I was so easily depressed. An aspiring actress who dealt with rejection on a regular basis. Lotte and Lili were my antidepressants. I had felt internationalized by being included in their romp.

"And Yanni?" I ask, still using the Greek pronunciation. "He was Lili's cousin, right?"

"Married the daughter of a Greek shipping magnate like his father—as he was supposed to."

"Oh right, I did know that. He took me to the best New Year's party I would ever attend," I say. "A night filled with grandparents, children, children of children, friends blending in with his family, moussaka, wine and music. No New Year's Eve has ever lived up to that night. I slept with him you know. Oh, but not on that night."

It is Lotte's turn to stop walking. "You did?" she says, clearly surprised. "Michael was the first man I ever slept with!"

This shocks me almost as much as Lili's suicide. "But . . ." is all I can manage to get out. All the men I'd gone to bed with believing I was catching up to her, and all along Lotte had been a virgin? I wonder if there were others after Michael. She did say he was her first.

We have reached my hotel.

"So, we'll see you at 6:30," she says. More a statement than a question.

"Of course! Looking forward to it, I lie. I would much prefer to continue talking, filling in the blanks. "You know I could come with you now and help," I tell her. "I am a great sous chef." But she gives me a kiss on each cheek and takes off. The puzzle left unfinished.

Her handwriting on the onion skin sheets of paper mostly undecipherable. The return address somewhere in Europe. She'd taken up numerology. 'You must add a T to your name. . .Will change your life.' I repeated her words to an actor friend. He went and bought a large Tiffany T on a chain with my first name imprinted on it. It hung it around my neck until my father demanded I take it off. We are Jewish and it looked like a cross.

Their apartment is small. There is little or no art. What décor there is, lacks interest. What happened? She'd studied design. Graduated from art school. Had I ever seen her drawings? I search my memory. Then a page of quick sketches comes to mind. Fashion drawings. Figures posed in all directions. In ink. They were good.

Michael is in a chair near the window. He's overweight, slovenly, dressed in a large white T-shirt and grey shorts. He appears drunk. From the stroke? From liquor? He doesn't get up. Maybe it's too difficult.

"You remember Margo," Lotte says.

"Had to get your approval to marry her, didn't I?" he bellows. Whatever charm there'd been is now gone.

"I'm sure not," I say.

"Took you to dinner," he adds.

"Yes, I remember."

A few more exchanges, and Lotte helps Michael to the table. There's no cocktail hour. It's dinner as usual. He sits at the head. Lotte stays standing. She serves.

"When did you two meet?" he queries though it sounds more like a command.

"All yours," I say to Lotte, hoping a piece will fall into place.

"When we were 19, Michael," she sounds like a mother tired of answering a four-year old's incessant questions. "I was at Parson's and Margo at the Playhouse."

And suddenly I'm standing on the steps outside my school, Lotte and a group of her classmates are milling around on the sidewalk. It is after a production I'd been in. Which one I have no idea. Her hair is cut short. She's wearing a cashmere sweater set, a wool plaid skirt that falls just below her knees. I assume she has on pumps with Cuban heels—it was the late fifties. But then what, I wonder. What came next?

I watch Lotte place slices of brisket on each of our plates, followed by mashed potatoes and peas—foods I think of as part of my childhood, not my present life. She cuts Michael's meat into bite size pieces, places the fork into his hand and sits. We work at conversation.

"You know I have a T in my name now," I say. "Even made it official. Just a middle letter "T" without a period after it."

"And life got better, yes?" she says as if a given.

I leave out how long it took for it even to be passable.

"I'm flying out to see my brother in Fairbanks next week," she says. "A friend will stay with Michael."

I want to ask why he's in Alaska, but I think she'd told me this at some point. I daren't ask about her parents as I have no memory as to whether they're alive or dead. The evening, while short in length, feels endless. I return to the hotel and wonder where the woman I knew had gone. Or if I'd ever taken the time to know her.

She stood in my loft. Her long fingers played on her temples like a spider weaving a web. "I must lie down," she said, traces of Garbo punctuating her words. "Another headache?" I asked. She nodded and walked gingerly to the small so-called guest-room in the back of my loft, closing the door on my cat who wanted to join her. The room faced a sunless courtyard. As dark as it was, I heard her pull down the shade. I assumed it will be hours before she emerged. She'd already told me that she'd had to lock herself up in her hotel room for the past few days. Only ventured out to see me. I knew nothing about migraines; she looked perfectly fine to my uneducated eye. I tried to appear concerned. In truth, I was disbelieving, annoyed.

The phone rings. The caller ID says Alaska. The voice on the other end of the phone introduces herself as Lotte's sister-in-law. She explains that she's calling people whose name and number she'd found in Lotte's address book. She conveys the news that Lotte has died. They'd brought her to Fairbanks when she was first diagnosed so she wouldn't be alone. Breast cancer. Spread quickly. Gone in six months. "Are there other friends you know whom we should call?" the sister-in-law asks. I explain that it's been at least six or seven years since we'd been in touch and the only person that I knew to be a friend of Lotte's, Peter Prescott the food critic, had also died. I extend my condolences, thank her for the call, and we say goodbye.

I don't cry. Simply walk to the microwave to heat up my coffee—something I do whenever I don't know where to place myself. Then the tears start. I force myself to stop. Remind myself how we'd not spoken in years. And that we hadn't been real friends even longer. But the tears want to flow interrupted by sobs. The more I try to push away my feelings of loss, the harder they push back. I go to the closet and pull out the soft, warm nightshirt she had sent me after that last visit. One I'm not even certain I thanked her for as it made me feel extremely inadequate–aware that I couldn't return her affection. Later I slip it on and wear it to bed.

The French Lesson

"Excuse me," a woman's voice cut through the din of gallery goer's chatter. "Are you Janet?"

Her newly refreshed wine glass in hand, Janet turned to see an attractive woman, somewhere around her own age, with very little makeup, small diamond studs in the ears, in a black silk sheath with a floppy rose made from the same fabric pinned on. "I am," she answered, glad that at the last minute she herself had added a colorful scarf to what she usually wore to openings—a black top, black pleated skirt, and heels.

"Jeanine said we should meet. Well really, that I should meet you. Michele Fountaine," the woman said extending her hand then withdrawing it as she noticed the glass in Karen's.

Janet glanced over to where Jeanine was standing, but Jeanine's attention was elsewhere. "Any specific reason?"

"She thought I might pick your brain."

Janet couldn't make out the accent. "Don't know how much of my brain there is to be picked."

"Obviously Jeanine thinks there's plenty. . . A bit more red please," the woman said handing her own glass to the young man behind the bar table as if she needed fortification before continuing. Then turning back to Janet, "You see my husband and I are in the States for the next two years and oh, it's way too long to go into here. Would you let me take you to lunch sometime soon? Or, and I know this sounds a bit crazy, but if you're game, and as I'm famished and need to eat, we could grab a bite around the corner no—on me, of course. Unless you already have plans."

Between Janet's aching feet and her own rumbling stomach the thought of sitting down appealed. Besides, one never knew where Jeanine's constant shuffling people like cards in a deck could lead. "Well that would certainly save me from trying to make something out of an empty fridge. There's a café up the block. Reasonable food."

"Oh, that's wonderful," Michele said.

Janet hoped she hadn't made a mistake by accepting.

"I can't make out the accent," Janet said after they'd each put in their order of a hamburger, French fries, and a glass of wine—white for Janet, red for Michele.

"I'm originally from Minneapolis but have lived in France for many years. And as we, that's my husband and I, travel so much, I'm not sure what I sound like anymore."

"Inscrutable," Janet said hoping it would be taken as a compliment. "How long have you lived in France?"

"Twenty-five, well, twenty-six years to be exact."

"Really!" Janet knew people who had come to New York to seek whatever and stayed, but none who'd left the States for good. "I'm not sure I'd ever be able to move to another country," she said. "Not that I haven't thought about it those times I was abroad and carried away by the romance of wherever I was or whomever I was with. But I always returned home."

The waiter interrupted with their wine. "Ah bon," Michele said, both women perfunctorily clicking glasses before taking their first sips.

"And your husband? French? American?"

"French"

"Well that explains the twenty-five years. What does he do?" The interviewer in her taking over.

"He's a TV newscaster. We call them présentateurs du JT. And you, married?"

"No. Beaucoup affairs de le coeur, but no husbands. Did I say that right?"

"Affaires de cœur—no 'le'. Very courageous of you. I've only been with one man."

Grateful to see the waiter heading towards them with their food, Janet could only smile. They clearly were in two very different worlds.

"I am not sure I would be this open if we were sitting in Paris," the woman continued. "There's a freedom to being here. Paris can be a very small town."

"Trust me, so can New York."

"Were you born here?"

"Born and bred."

"Of course! Who leaves New York?"

"You!"

"I left Minneapolis. Not the same thing."

"True. So, what brain picking did you want to do?"

A deep inhalation of air then on one breath, "I would love to learn more about how you conduct interviews and perhaps watch you at work if at all possible."

"Are you a writer?"

"No. No. But I've been thinking that if I could interview women here who have different types of careers, maybe I could create a podcast? Something for people back home."

"I see."

"To be completely honest, I really need to be working at something, what with my kids on their own, my husband always busy. And when I mentioned this to Jeanine—a mutual friend gave me her name when she knew I was coming over—she thought you'd be a great person to start with."

Janet couldn't quite figure out this woman. On the one hand she seemed worldly, assured, on the other incredibly verdant, even fragile. "Not sure what I could tell you except to be extraordinarily curious. As for the writing, there are plenty of courses you could take while you're here. Gotham has a slew."

"I think Jeanine meant that perhaps you could perhaps suggest women I might talk with, then work with me on putting it together."

Janet motioned with her hand that she needed to finish the food in her mouth before answering. Clearly the woman meant to pay and additional income, even small, wouldn't hurt. But she had a deadline looming on an article. And who knew how much would be required of her. But before she could answer the woman said, "Think about it. In the meantime, we're having a party next Saturday evening at our home. Can I entice you? It'll be a very eclectic group. Most everyone we know are transplants like ourselves."

Janet couldn't remember the last time she'd been to a party in someone's home. None of her friends gave parties anymore. And her life certainly had gotten way too predictable. A new group of people not attached to the art world might be just what she needed to spice things up. "I would love to come," she said. "Thank you." She would have to remember to thank Jeanine.

"Come meet the rest of our guests," Michele said, wrapping her arm around Janet's and pulling her away from Hugo, who bowed his head as if tipping a hat in farewell. "My husband can monopolize."

Janet had no choice but to follow. A shame really. She'd found Hugo more than a little attractive. His chiseled face, his expressive hands with their long-articulated fingers right out of a Da Vinci study. Then again, just as well. Not only was he taken, but she knew the wife.

"I hope you didn't mention what we talked about, did you?" Michele asked, her voice low.

"No. Is it a secret?"

"I'll explain later." Michele brought Janet over to a couple who were staring at a painting near the bookcase. "Andrea and Pierre, meet our newest acquisition, Janet. She writes about art and artists. And Janet, Vikki and Pierre collect. You all should have lots to talk about." And with that introduction, Michele moved on to see to her other guests, her long shiny, straight black hair swaying ever so slightly leaving a tinge of envy in her wake.

"And what would you write about this painting?" demanded Andrea as her hand gestured towards the work in question. The ring on her finger sending flashes of light onto the rather mundane seascape.

"I'd have to be more immersed in the artist's work before I could begin to write anything," Janet demurred, not wanting to make a negative comment regarding her hosts' taste—grateful enough for having been invited.

Not letting up Andrea countered with, "Shouldn't good art be recognized upon sight?"

"But art is so personal, isn't it?" Janet's gallery smile plastered on. "It's as much in the eye of the beholder as the work itself, no?" She used the excuse that she needed more ice for her drink to escape to the far corner of the room where the food and drinks were laid out.

"So, how do you know the Fountaines?" an attractive man asked peering over his glasses that rested low on his nose just as Janet added the unnecessary ice cube to her scotch in case Andrea was watching. His non-descript pairing of a navy jacket, blue shirt and khaki pants not giving off a clue as to what he did. She took him to be about ten years younger than herself— age having become somewhat of a fixation as her 50th loomed.

"Met Michele last week at a gallery opening" she replied, transferring her glass to her left hand, and extending her right. "Janet Winfred."

"Philippe Dors." He held her hand a few seconds longer than necessary before releasing it. "So, you're an art lover."

She resisted wanting to remove his glasses. He certainly didn't use them. "That implies I love all art and I don't. How do you know our hosts?"

"Hugo and I work together."

"Then you're a TV newsman. A, oh what did she call it, ah yes, a présentateur du JT."

"Very good. No, I'm behind the scenes. Producer. He's on camera."

"And are you also from Paris?" It had been a long time since a man whose eyes showed an enticing intellect had come on to her. A long time since any man had come on to her for that matter.

"And I will assume you're from New York."

"Guilty . . . Your English is flawless."

"Just good with languages."

Janet could feel her whole body begin to respond. "Michele said they planned to be here for at least two more years. The same for you?"

"That's what we signed on for. But you never know. Why don't I fix us something. What would you like?" Philippe said as he began to fill a plate with shrimps, a chunk of brie, and crackers. "Something else?" he asked.

Janet forwent the vegetables she would have opted for, shook her head no, and followed him to a sofa just under the window. He waited for her to sit then set the plate of food down next to her as he unfolded himself onto the cushion, one leg half up on the sofa, the other stretched out on the floor. Smart, she thought. Not too close, but close enough.

"So, then, what do you do," he asked seeming to be truly interested. Another rarity.

"I write. Mostly commentary on artists and the art world." It was all beginning to feel a bit like foreplay.

"He's not very interesting once you know him, you know."

"Who?"

"Hugo. I noticed how taken you were when you were talking with him."

"I was just being polite."

"We won't argue so soon."

She laughed. "You plan for us to argue down the line?" Definitely foreplay.

"I rewrite most of his scripts. He says my words. Repeats them at parties."

"Wow. Jealous?"

"Not in the least. Just stating facts."

"Not sure I believe you," her tone returning his tease. "Do Hugo and Michelle give these parties a lot?" she asked.

"Often enough. Ex-pats bond together. Most of the people in the room are either from our embassy, are journalists of one sort or another, plus some business types, like the two you were talking to.

"You were following me?"

"You weren't a familiar face and as they usually invite an American or two, to remind themselves what country they're in, I assumed you were that person." He scooped a bit of brie onto a cracker and held it out to her. "New faces are always welcome," a smile playing around his mouth.

Janet swallowed what he'd offered, clenching the muscles in her stomach and thighs. It had been two years since she'd been to bed with anyone let alone an attractive, teasing Frenchman.

"Did you sleep with him?" Michele asked when Janet called the next day to thank her for the party.

Janet didn't know how to answer, not certain whether she broke some cardinal rule about going off with a guest of Michele's.

"Well good for you if you did," Michele continued. "There are times I wish I were single again and this time take advantage of being so."

"I'm sure not. You two are quite the couple."

"Trust me, marriage isn't easy. Listen, how about brunch on Sunday? Hugo must leave at the crack of dawn on an assignment. We could discuss how to work together."

"Could we make it a bit later in the day?" Janet said wanting to keep the morning open just in case Philippe returned to her bed Saturday night—a languid morning of sex something she hadn't experienced in years.

"Of course," Michele said. "By the way, Philippe usually goes with Hugo. They're a pair. But later is fine. How about mid-afternoon."

Even with Michele professing to give her a thumb's up for sleeping with Philippe, Janet wasn't ready to offer up a "caught me" and opt for the brunch. The relationship too new. So, she simply said she'd be there at 4. And with that, she attempted to focus her attention on the day ahead, and not the possibility of the phone ringing with Philippe on the other end.

"I must say," Janet's eyes once again taking in the apartment, "I envy the amount of space you have." Her own one-bedroom on the upper west side standing in sharp contrast to the Fontaine's three bedroom, two and a half baths on Sutton Place. The two women were curled up, shoes off, feet up, like facing book ends on either ends of the sofa—a plate of cookies between them.

"The Network owns it and most everything in it. We could never afford this. The photographs and throw pillows are ours from home. I packed a slew of them. It helps."

"So, the art on the walls?" Janet trying to keep any hints of judgment out of her voice then breathing a sigh of relief when Michele answered.

"Dieu no! Why was Vikki doing her 'I know great art when I see it' routine?"

"I escaped her before she got that far."

"May I ask you something?"

"Of course, and yes, I've slept with him." There! It was out. Janet having wanted to talk to Michele about Philippe from the moment she'd arrived.

"That wasn't what I was going to ask, but ..."

"Oh, I thought . . ." Janet's cheeks turning red.

Michelle's hand waved off Janet's concerns. "As I said on the phone, I'm fine with that. No, what I was going to ask is what you would think if I, we, did what we talked about not as podcasts, but as a series for French TV? Maybe I could even be on camera doing the interviews. Thoughts?"

Janet stared at her host. She certainly was more than attractive. Had a distinctive manner about her. Showed curiosity. "Have you ever interviewed anyone?"

"That's what I would need you to teach me. At least the basics."

"I don't understand why you're not discussing this with Hugo and Philippe. I mean it's more their world than mine."

"No!" Michele cried practically jumping off the sofa, her body taut, her arms straight at her sides. She looked to Janet like a child screaming for attention. "Because I want to be the one doing the interviewing, and they won't take me seriously unless I prove I can do it."

"I get it," Janet said in an attempt to calm Michele down. "It's okay," the change in Michele's demeanor coming as a total surprise. "Michele," Janet's voice lowering, almost in a whisper. "Would you like me to introduce you to some women I know? Maybe some artists?"

And just as quickly as Michele had appeared on the verge of splintering into pieces, she regained her composure, launching into what clearly was a well-thought out list of wants: "Yes, please. And I would like you to work with me. Let me watch you interview artists. I wouldn't be in competition with you, because you don't do TV and it wouldn't be for American audiences. I could pay you a modest amount up front only because I don't want Hugo suspecting, but if it sells, then of course whatever you think fair." She stood frozen as if her life depended on Janet's reaction.

Janet took her time responding. "I could certainly put together a list for you. Even make some introductions. What if we start there. How about we decide on a modest, using your word, hourly rate? Would that work?"

Michele's smile came back on. "Bon! I need a drink. White for you, yes? Or perhaps something stronger?"

Janet had the key in her lock as the phone went off.

"Again, you promise you will not mention this to Philippe, yes?" It was clear by the way Michele over-enunciated her words that she'd continued to drink after Janet had left.

"I promise."

"Did I tell you, you're lucky you never married."

"Michele, I just walked in the door. Can we save this for another time?"

"Didn't you ever want to get married," Michele asked as she beat the egg for their omelet almost to the breaking point. Another Sunday with Hugo and Philippe on assignment.

Janet hated the question and decided to change her usual answer of 'just never met the right man' to something slightly closer to the truth. "Poor choices, I guess."

"You see Philippe as a poor choice?"

Janet roared. "You are sounding like my old shrink. Didn't expect that from you."

"Well, is he?"

"He's a fabulous bed partner."

"Bien! If that's all he is, then maybe you'll lend him to me sometime and you could take Hugo." The look of shock on Janet's face must have surprised Michele, for she immediately followed up with, "Only making a joke. I am not serious. Vraiment. Truly, joking."

"You won't believe what Michele asked," Janet said, her legs wrapped around Philippe's.

"Quoi," reverting to his native tongue when spent.

"She wants me to lend you to her. More than that, that we switch."

"Qu'est-ce-que tu as dit?"

"I told her to leave her hands off you. Do you mind?"

"Pas de tout. And you? Hands off Hugo? Or are you still curious," waking up to the subject.

"Of course not. Never was. But are you 'curious' about Michele?" She could feel her stomach knot up.

"Most men are "curious' about every woman they meet."

Her throat tightened. "That's not answering my question."

"I have no desire to have sex with Michele or have you in bed with Hugo. Now, dormi."

A shiver went through Janet's body and she pressed closer.

"That was anything but one of my best," Janet said as she and Michele left the studio. Janet's usual ability to carry on an interview without any awareness of self, had felt staged as if she was outside herself directing every move, even though Michele had remained silent in the back of the loft—the only sound that of her pen scratching on paper as she took notes. "It felt forced. I don't know what came over me."

"But I learned a lot, ma cherie. Honest."

"What you should have learned is what not to do. That question, 'And did you always want to be an artist?' Terrible! The last thing you want is to elicit a yes or no response."

"I distracted you."

"I should not have been distracted. I think the best thing for you to do is take the list I gave you and start doing a few interviews on your own. Record them and we can dissect them later. How's that?" She had wanted to show off to Michele and clearly had failed.

"Bien! That's what I'll do. Again, not a word."

"Oh, for God's sake! Michele. I promised. Enough!"

And Janet kept to her word. When Philippe asked what she and Michele had done on a particular day, she lied and said they'd shopped. When the two couples—for now Janet and Philippe were considered a couple—were out for dinner, she didn't let it slip. Not even after she'd consumed two glasses of wine and Hugo had teased Michele for not having sought a career. Nor when, as he had last night, become uncharacteristically snide and Janet wanted to jump in to defend her friend. But Michele's warning look had stopped her from doing so.

"What was that all about?" Janet asked, their morning calls over coffee now a ritual.

"Bad patch," Michele's sadness verging on despair coming through the phone.

"Sounded more than that. Is there anything I can do?" It hurt to see Michele in this much pain.

"Marriage is not easy. I've tried to tell you that."

"I am so sorry. What are you going to do? I mean that was pretty bad."

"Work on my presentation. C'est tout."

A week later the roles reversed.

"He's leaving," Janet sobbed into the phone. "Just like that. He told me over breakfast, like he was discussing eggs."

"I heard that was a possibility but did not have the heart to tell you. But you knew this would end, yes?"

"Not so soon!" she hated what her shrink had called 'her pattern.' Her diving into passionate affairs that she knew from the beginning were destined to end. Then, no matter how she convinced herself that she could keep herself intact, inevitably she began imagining they would go on forever or at least, in Philippe's case, a few years. But no, out of the blue he's called back. Worse, he accepted the new post without question. No haggling with the bosses. No discussing it with her. Just 'We knew this would end eventually. Only means it's come sooner than we expected.' She'd found herself screaming, 'How long have you known? How could you not have said something?' Her pain wrenching out of her body. The sex that night mindless as the rational part of her dissolved.

"Oh, ma petite, do you want to meet for lunch? Or a drink later?" Michele asked, her condolences only adding to Janet's misery.

"I don't know what I want. No, I do," she bawled." I want him here! Oh God, let me talk to you later, okay?" And with that Janet took to her bed, in a fetal position, a pillow pressed to her stomach.

"I don't know where to start, but I have news." They were back on Michele's sofa. Well, Janet was seated. Michele was nervously prancing about.

It was the first morning that Janet had awoken in a decent mood. "Okay, shoot!"

"Now please, don't get mad at me. I had wanted to tell you, but I thought I'd be doing more harm if I kept talking about Philippe, so I kept quiet. And it was your idea for me to discuss it with him."

"What are you talking about?"

"Philippe presented my series up to the Network and they are interested. So much so, they're flying me back. Can you imagine?"

For a moment Janet found it hard to breath. The scent of betrayal overwhelming. Somehow, she managed, "I thought Philippe wasn't supposed to know." The bile in her chest rising. "Well, once he was back in France, I emailed him, and he began to work with me."

"Was this before or after you stopped asking me for advice?"

"Does it matter? I always said if it sells, I'd pay you."

Janet turned cold. "Does Hugo know?"

"We've told him."

"You and Philippe are now a 'we'?"

"You know what I mean."

"No, Michele, I don't. Tell me, are you planning on sleeping with him?"

Janet watched Michele's cheeks turn red. Her, "No, of course not!" not at all believable.

Janet stood up and in a voice reeking with sarcasm, did a dead-on imitation of the woman who up to that moment she'd begun to consider a close friend. "Oh, ma chère, I'm only joking, vraiment. What crap! Maybe I should sleep with Hugo. Though the way you were looking to get into bed with Philippe, Hugo's probably lousy. But then you wouldn't know having only supposedly slept with one man, would you?" And with that Janet retrieved her coat from the hall closet, picked up her bag and saw herself out. If she'd overreacted, so be it. She'd had enough with the French.

Dead Daisies Strewn All Over

No matter that it's past 11 at night, she picks up the phone, her fingers shaking so violently she misses the holes. She tries three more times until she can dial all the way through. —How could you not tell me? she blasts as her mother picks up. —I had to hear it on the news? —I thought I'd tell you in the morning, her mother says. —I wanted you to have a good night's sleep. It is such a ludicrous comment that she doesn't know whether to laugh or to cry. She hangs up and out from her gut comes an agonized howl.

They were cousins—born three months apart. It was expected they would be friends forever. But they were sent to different schools, different camps, and rarely saw each other. She remembers her mother showing her a picture of the two of them sitting in a sandbox each with their own pail and shovel. Even then it was as if the other didn't exist.

When she turned 16, she and her parents moved across town into the same building, the same apartment directly below where her cousin and her parents lived. —Go upstairs and visit, her mother urged soon after they settled in. —Shouldn't she have welcomed me? her retort. —At least a phone call? —It's nice to have a friend in the building. Her mother insisted. —Go!

Her aunt opened the door. —She's in her room with friends from

from school. I'm sure she'll be happy for you to join them. Go in. You know where it is.

Her cousin's room surprised. There was a real bed, a desk for homework, and even posters on the wall. A girl's room so different from her own. Her cousin and her friends seemed to talk in code giggling, whispering. She found them childish. Alien. She made her excuses and quickly returned to her own room downstairs decorated to look like a den. Her desk hidden in a bookcase. Her bed designed to look like a sofa. It was where her father often played cards with his friends.

Years passed. Her cousin took up photography in Israel. She, herself, worked as a sculptor in New York. They hadn't kept in touch, so she was surprised when her cousin, visiting from Tel Aviv, called to say she'd like to stop by. Turned out to be a condolence call. —Why didn't your father leave you something? her cousin had demanded as they ate the lunch she'd prepared. —There wasn't anything to leave, she'd explained. —Mom needs it all. —But not even a letter? A token? Her cousin incredulous. —Of course, not, she'd answered. She couldn't imagine her father leaving a note or a token. It was enough he seemed to appreciate her caretaking before he died. —How long are you staying this time? she asked her cousin. —Not long, her cousin said. —I'm only here to make out a will. —Really? The idea of having a will at their age seemed weird. Not that she would have had a penny to leave anyway. —Are you ever returning to the States? she asked. —Maybe next year, her cousin answered. They spent over an hour together yet never discussed art or photography.

The next year her cousin, back in town, called to say she'd landed a one-woman show at the Jewish museum. —Congratulations, she said trying not to let her shock and resentment find their way into her voice. —Thanks, her cousin responded. —Listen, do you know someone with a darkroom? I'm in desperate need of one. —She offered to make some calls. When she called back to tell her cousin she'd found one, she asked if they could get together for coffee. Mostly she was curious as to how the show had come about. She herself had yet to secure a dealer or a gallery and she'd been at it way longer than her cousin —Don't think I'll have time, her cousin had said. —But I'll see you at the opening, yes? —Of course, she'd answered, wishing she could find an excuse to stay away.

It was a large square room. Her cousin's photographs, enlarged and expensively mounted, lining the walls. There were red dots everywhere. She forced herself to look at the work finding only one of interest. She knew she wasn't succeeding in feigning happiness for her cousin's success and she left as soon as she reasonably could.

The newscaster's voice plays over and over in her head. "The body on the beach outside of Tel Aviv was identified today as the photographer . . ."

At Shiva she was told that her cousin had left her money in her will. —She was angry that your father didn't leave you anything, her aunt said. Her voice cold. Her eyes ice. —Dad didn't have enough to leave. Mom needed everything. I tried to explain that to her. —So did I, her aunt mumbled and walked away.

She attended Shiva every day. Her aunt ignored her. She finally got up the courage to ask her aunt what she'd done wrong. —I will never forget that sour look on your face at her show. I will never forget it! She was certain that her aunt wanted to slap her across the face. She almost wished she had. —I am so sorry, she said. —Really, truly sorry. And trying not to be too graphic, she described the difficult year she'd had. One disappointment after another. One sickness after another. She admitted to being resentful, even envious. Her aunt seemed to accept her apology and she used the inherited money to cast three pieces in bronze asking her aunt to choose one for herself. Her aunt picked the smallest.

Years later, her aunt will ask what she would like for her 50th and she will describe the piece she remembered from the show:

a mass of yellow Crown Daisies uprooted, blowing in the wind against a desert landscape. —I would love to hang it across from my bed. It will be the first thing I'll see every morning and the last before going to sleep. Her aunt will not say anything. She won't need to. The slight softening of her eyes will say it all.

Finding Home

"Just buzz me in!" Julia yelled into the intercom in response to Esther's, "Finally!" clearly meant to admonish Julia's lateness. The buzzer released the door and Julia switched out of her heels to the flats she kept in her tote. Besides the shoes, the bag contained her laptop, makeup, keys, and a slew of unnecessary items she rarely travelled anywhere without. She grabbed onto the railing and steeled herself for the climb ahead. When she'd lived here with Esther, unbelievably over some 40 years ago, she could race up and down the stairs without a thought, often practicing her ball/heel on each step to the consternation of their neighbors. It was dingy then, even more so now. For Esther's sake she wished the landlord would at least paint the halls. "I'm coming," she yelled, shaking off the familiar wave of nostalgia as she started up the stairs—her limp barely perceptible.

"How the hell do you still do this?" Julia managed to wheeze out, stopping on the floor below Esther's to use her inhaler. "No wonder you haven't gained a pound." She herself had put on a good ten. "I should never have smoked."

"Do it enough times a day and one doesn't need a gym," Esther called down in that throaty actor voice of hers.

"If I had the time, I'd get there more often," Julia mumbled and pulled herself up the last flight.

"Well, if it makes you feel any better, the stairs are not as easy for me as they used to be either."

When Julia finally made it through the door, she plopped down onto one of the three kitchen chairs placed around the table, all four pieces rescued from the street. "For you," Julia said reaching into her tote and pulling out a small package.

"We're only having a tiny dessert," Esther said refusing to take the box from Julia's outstretched hand. "I come to you empty handed almost all the time."

"It's not a care package for God's sake! It's a regift that I won't use and thought you'd like." She placed the box on the table.

"In that case, thank you. And if I can't use it, I'll regift it as well. No note inside, I assume."

"None that I know of." It was an old story. Esther's gift to a friend that had made the rounds only to come back to her a year later, her original note still inside.

Having caught her breath, Julia took off her coat and hung it in the closet while Esther poured coffee into Julia's favorite mug—adding a splash of milk with two packets of Splenda. "Thanks," Julia said, taking it and the linzertortes into the living room. Esther following with her mint tea and napkins.

The two women settled onto the sofa, one on either end, shoes off, legs pulled under, coffee, tea and torte in hand. It was their monthly ritual usually held at Julia's. This time Esther had insisted on her place and Julia had acquiesced. She covered herself with the old afghan throw from the back of the sofa—the 56 degree temperature outside keeping the heat from being turned on even though it was the second week in October—while Esther rewrapped her heavy black wool sweater more tightly around her body. Actually, it was Julia's sweater. One she'd passed on to Esther a few years back. "Bought by mistake. Way too long for me and I can't return it. Besides you live in black," Julia had said. And Esther had followed with an overly dramatic, "I'm in mourning for my life, I am very unhappy" –one of her favorite Chekhovian lines.

How had they lived together Julia wondered as she looked around the room—her own apartment a study in minimalism. Still if she overlooked the climb, she enjoyed being here. The sofa old but cushiony. The montage of different periods and styles that Esther chose to surround herself with—whether they went together or not—oddly pleasing. 'Eclectic Design,' Esther called it.

"So, what's new?" Julia asked. Their schedules rarely allowing for even phone catchups nowadays.

"You start," Esther said

And Julia filled Esther in on the two miserable Match.com dates, "The worst!" Her nephew's new business venture, "I hope I don't lose what monies I gave him," and an update on her brother's drinking problem, 'Don't ask!" She left out that she'd been given a new title and a raise. Esther already knew she was successful. No need to pile it on. "Your turn!" She sensed it wouldn't be good news. Esther looked strained. Her normal thinness verging on gaunt.

"I'm going to have to move," Esther said in a voice without inflection. "Landlord selling the building."

If Esther was going for maximum effect by downplaying the awfulness of the situation—something they were taught to do in drama class—she had more than achieved her goal. All Julia could get out was an, "Oh my God. . . Esther. . . Why didn't you call me?"

"You were travelling. Figured I'd tell you when I saw you."

This was no act, Julia decided. Esther was simply trying to keep it together. "Did you know this was coming?"

"Seems he stopped renewing leases a year ago, but as there were still three of us rent stabilized tenants, I figured we were safe. Then the older couple downstairs—don't you love me calling them "older" when they're probably only ten to fifteen years our senior? Anyway, they decided to move to be closer to their children. And Karl, across the hall—with great apologies to me I should add—decided to take the buyout. He'd been wanting to get out of New York ever since Freda died. I think you met them, yes? Anyway, that left me."

"What was the buyout?" Julia asked watching her friend twist

her long auburn hair up into a bun, then let it fall then twist it again. Julia had cut her own off years ago. Easier.

"Not enough for someone to stay in New York indefinitely. I know legally I can't be forced out, but he could make my life miserable. Start construction around me. Take me to court knowing I don't have the money to fight him for any length of time. And because I see students here, he could say that I'm running a business from my home. Aren't you glad you left this life?"

"I had no choice, remember?" Julia snapped. The memory of lying flat out on the curb, her leg mangled from the cab that had hit her, not totally erased even after all these years.

"You could have continued acting. There was more to life than musicals, Julia. And you were damn good."

"Don't change the subject. Back to you, please. Es, have to ask, how are you moneywise?"

"Same as always," spoken in a flat, resigned voice.

Actors are basically masochists, Julia thought. The incessant search for work. Auditioning over and over again only to be rejected because one's hair was the wrong color or one's nose not quite right. The constant dredging up of emotions. Not to mention the willingness to satisfy a director's vision whether you agreed with it or not. "Do you have any idea of what you're going to do?" she asked as gently as possible.

"Not a clue. Love those successful actors who say it's a good thing they made it because acting is the only thing they can do. Acting—and teaching acting along with Pilates—are the only things I can do, so why the hell didn't I make it? Sorry. Swore I wouldn't let this become a pity party. You wouldn't want a roommate, would you?"

Julia's momentary panic was quelled by Esther's, "Don't worry, I'm kidding."

"Wasn't worried," she lied. "Anyway, I thought it can take up to six months to evict someone."

"Probably, but I will still have to figure out what comes after. Is that new?" Esther asked her eyes having fallen on Julia's bracelet.

Instinctively Julia's hand went under the throw. She shouldn't have worn it.

"You don't have to hide it," Esther said. "Let me see."

And Julia extended her arm to show the gold cuff with tiny set-in red stones.

"Wear it well."

"Thank you," she said pulling back from Esther's hand. "Do you have a lawyer?"

Esther shook her head.

"I'll check with mine for you. Okay? And if you haven't found a place by the time you have to leave, then of course, you'll stay with me until you do." Immediately she berated herself for making it sound so open ended. It rankled that Esther hadn't taken better care of herself. The grandfather clock in the corner a perfect example of one of Esther's extravagances. "You spent what?" she remembered saying in astonishment as two of their friends carried it through the door. "I couldn't pass it up," Es had replied. "It was only $500." The 'only' happening to be Esther's salary that week for a cameo on a soap and she'd blown it on an antique grandfather clock when their rent was due in a week's time. Well maybe today it could bring enough to cover the two-months security on an apartment. That is, if grandfather clocks were even in demand.

They spent another hour or so with Julia coming up with ideas, perhaps applying to Westbeth—an artist's residence—and Esther countering with "There's a waiting list a mile long just to get into the lottery." Or that Esther look into out-of-town repertory companies only to be met with, "I can't start over in a new town now, just can't." Eventually Julia gave up, gathered her belongings, and said her good-byes, holding onto the railing as she made her way down the stairs—her emotions ricocheting between relief that she owned her own place, foreboding for Esther, and anger that Esther was in this predicament.

Whether Esther expected rescuing or not, Julia knew she'd have to be the one to help. Hadn't Esther stayed with her, sleeping in a chair every night by Julia's hospital bed. Then once home helping to pull Julia out of the overwhelming depression that took over as her mangled leg eviscerated her dreams. Nothing is free, Julia thought. Nothing comes without at least one string attached.

Esther washed out the cups, the empty plate of tortes mirroring how she felt. Living even for a few weeks with Julia held no appeal. It was one thing when they were on equal footing, but this would mean she'd be a guest—no worse, an interloper. She walked back into the living room. The thought of having to give away her possessions or put them in storage overwhelmed her. She curled up on the sofa, pressed one of the throw pillows against her stomach and tried to convince herself that she'd get through this. Hadn't she weathered plenty of rough patches before? Ones that at the time seemed insurmountable. Different. Through them all she'd had her home. A place she could crawl back to after a disastrous stint with a touring company, an emotionally debilitating breakup or during a fallow period when she'd been convinced, she'd never get a part again. Her home, this home had been her anchor. Now she'd be floating. Aimless.

A few days later Julia called. Her lawyer confirmed what Esther had thought. The landlord could stop her from having classes in her apartment even if she tried to disguise them as social get-togethers and the constant harassment would leave her depleted in more ways than one. The lawyer did offer to represent Esther at half his normal fee. "I'll pay him now and you can pay me back whenever," Julia's tone decisive.

"Every penny," Esther said while wishing Julia would just charge the lawyer's fees to her business, take it as a tax write-off or however one handles those things. She forced herself not to think of what that bracelet must have cost.

About a week or so later, Esther heard a commotion in the hall and opened her door to see the moving men carting her neighbor Karl's furniture away. She was about to close her door when he appeared a piece of paper in his hand.

"I was just coming over. Hoped you'd be home," he said remnants of a German accent still there. "Wanted you to have my address and all. Do you know what's happening yet for you?"

Esther shook her head, her eyes beginning to fill with tears.

"Hey, it'll work out," Karl said. A big burly man with a soft voice, he put his arms around her. She allowed herself to nestle into his body, let him envelop her like a thick comforter. She had knocked on his and Freda's door more than once over the years. The back and forth kept to a minimum in the beginning, sometimes asking for help to open a jar, or Freda to zip up a dress she couldn't do herself. The interactions only becoming more frequent when Freda took sick. Yet other than giving him a hug when Freda died, this was the first time their bodies had touched. She forced herself to straighten up.

"Come in a second," she said, taking his hand and leading him into the living room. "I want you to have something for your new home. I'm not going to be able to take most of it with me and I'd rather have things in the hands of people I know than fingered by strangers at a thrift shop."

"You love all of this," he said. His brown eyes not glancing away from hers.

"I mean it. What would you like?" She began walking around the room, touching one clock, then another, a small wooden Punch and Judy, skipping over the glass figurine that she'd slipped into her pocket the last night of Glass Menagerie. "What appeals?"

"No, you should keep everything. You'll find another place."

"Please!"

"All right then. Maybe a clock. You have so many." He too began to walk around. She noticed he'd lost a few pounds. Looked younger. More vibrant. "One with an alarm. I will keep it next to my bed."

Was he hitting on her? Now? After all this time? Granted the year after his wife died, he was in no state to think of someone else. But the day he's moving? His hands rested on one of her favorites. She wanted to scream, "Not that one," but bit her lip, smiled and said, "It has an alarm. But it's old so you'll have to wind it up." She watched his large fleshy hands cradle it. She desperately wanted them around her. "Would you like a drink before you go?"

"Let me run and give this to the movers to pack. They're almost finished. Then I'll be back with an open bottle of wine from the fridge."

It felt longer but had to be no more than a few minutes before he returned, put the bottle down, walked over, and drew her close. She could feel him harden against her.

Julia's first reaction when the flowers arrived was to call Esther and yell at her for spending money unnecessarily. Two dozen of Julia's favorite white lilies—vase included—with the note: 'How can I ever repay you?' written in Esther's own hand. But then, Julia more than deserved them, her lawyer having spent weeks wrestling out an arrangement with Esther's landlord that gave Esther five months to move, a buyout that would amount to a year's rent with a 10% increase, plus the lawyer's fees. The one stipulation, she'd have to put up with all the construction that would take place around her without complaint to which she'd readily agreed.

Julia placed the arrangement in the center of the parsons table behind the sofa—a space she left for flowers when she felt like a splurge, or if dinner company brought them instead of a bottle of wine. Whereas Esther relied on clutter for her apartment's cohesion, Julia's perfectly placed solitary objects strove and achieved a cool, calm look. She'd worked hard to achieve it.

"They're beautiful and thank you," Julia said when Esther picked up.

"Honest?"

"Honest and I won't even say you shouldn't have." Julia thought of inviting Esther over, changed her mind, then invited her anyway. "Want to come by? Have a drink. See them while they're still blooming?"

"You sure? Would love that."

"Of course, come on over. And don't bring anything! I've got plenty. See you here."

Mangled leg and all, Julia knew she'd had a head start having inherited her mom's one-bedroom apartment. But on the other hand, if she hadn't scrimped on the small pleasures, worked her way up the corporate ladder, putting up with all the machinations of office politics—not to mention the all-boys network— she'd never have been able to have the apartment she had today.

No, there was nothing to feel guilty about, she told herself. Nothing.

"You slept with whom?" Julia asked as she opened a bottle of wine—the crackers, cheese and veggies already on the counter. "Seriously? And you've kept this from me?"

"I don't tell you everything."

"Since when? How was it?"

"Amazingly good. And sad," Esther said settling herself on the bar stool.

"What could be sad? Christ! It's been four years since I bedded a man and God knows when it'll happen again." Julia loved the expression 'bedded.' So much better than screwed.

"He left for Maine the morning after," Esther said dipping a celery stick into the hummus. "I almost thought of packing up and going with him."

"That's a long way away to travel for sex, don't you think?"

"Well there'd be a roof over my head."

"You'll find something," Julia said trying to sound positive as much for Esther as herself. Not that Es didn't have other friends who could offer temporary shelter, but Julia knew hers would be the place. She shuddered to think it could be more than a few days. She was used to living alone. Had done so for so long that it had become a way of life—her early marriage only lasting a few years. Well, she certainly wasn't prepared at her age to have a roommate. Even the thought of someday needing a live-in aide horrified.

When Westbeth opened its lottery, Esther applied, though she had no desire to live in a building where only artists were housed. She thought of it as a ghetto. A place where artists could be kept separate from the rest of society. It didn't matter that the word artist covered the whole gamut from the visual arts to the written word to performers. She liked being "other." Being seen as different, perhaps even a bit odd. Her wardrobe, much like her apartment, a compendium of styles, colors, fabrics that perhaps wouldn't be put together in Vogue, but suited her well. She scoured Craig's List for rooms for rent, the website Street Easy for apartments, and registered with a real estate agent who looked at her askance when she told him what she could afford. She even researched a city program that helped the elderly with rent. But it stipulated that one couldn't earn over $50 thousand a year which meant if she landed another movie, or a show, she'd be out on the street again or living at Julia's. Her sleep became fitful, her mood swings wide, her emotions frayed. She got into the habit of calling Julia every morning, Julia making it clear she was worried and wanted her checking in.

"You're contemplating what?" Julia said. "Damn, you made me spill my coffee. Hold on . . . Okay, I'm back. Again, you plan to do what?"

"It's just an idea. I mean I only have a month left and nothing has opened up."

"Have you spoken to him since he left? I thought this was a one-night stand."

"We've spoken."

"How often?"

"Often." She stifled the urge to confess that she and Karl were now speaking every night as she lay in bed her body yearning for his.

"Are you crazy? Maine?"

"You were the one who suggested regional theater. He says there's a good company up there. And I can still look online for apartments. It's Maine not Borneo. He's got Wi-Fi. I checked. And if anything comes up, I'll be back down in a flash. Let's be honest. You don't want me moving into your place any more than I want to intrude on your life."

"What about your students? How are you going to earn money there? Besides, you hardly know the man for God's sake."

Knowing this could be Julia's reaction was exactly the reason she'd kept it from her. "I've known him for years just in a different way. Now I know he's good in bed. Besides, he's not letting me pay for anything so I will save on rent and can afford to put my stuff in storage."

"Not to mention that you haven't driven a car in how long?"

"He said it was like riding a bike."

"Like hell it is. At our age they start taking the keys away. You're having a mid-life crisis in your sixties."

"I'm not having a crisis. This is a crisis." She wished Julia would be supportive. She was frightened enough.

Julia was grateful that Esther's students had rallied around, helped Es pack and put most of her belongings into storage. Grateful that her own work had become so all-consuming she could focus on her life rather than Esther's. Besides, she had lived through Esther's other affairs, watched how she could morph into a new persona depending on whom she was with. Of course, when it ended and she returned o herself, she had her own home in which to grieve. Now she only had Julia's.

What with Karl apparently off doing some kind of country errand, she and Esther had one long Facetime call during which Esther gave her a tour of her new abode. "The only thing I can't show you is Karl in his blue T shirt and just-above-the-knee shorts—he's got great legs by the way—putting finishing touches on dinner while I'm in a frock setting the table."

Esther definitely was playing a role Julia thought, as Esther moved through the kitchen pointing the phone's camera on the rustic cabinets, the wood burning stove, old pots and pans hanging over a butcher block table and then into the living room with a rocking chair no less. Julia just hoped this made for TV Hallmark movie didn't turn into one where cabin fever sets in and the characters go mad. Or maybe run a scenario like the one Julia had watched one night when she was home alone feeling sorry for herself. City female lawyer finds love in a Maine village. Wrong! It was Alaska. Same difference. But Bullock didn't find love there, she took the guy from New York with her. And if Julia remembered correctly, they both returned to the city. Which means at some point she'd get a call and she'd have two houseguests until they could find a place to stay. No, only Esther would return because from the sound of it, there wasn't a crazy bone in Karl's body—definitely not Esther's type.

Weeks passed and reality began to set in. The pleasure of bucolic walks, sunsets on the beach, sex and more sex—even Karl's lobster bisque—could not compete with Esther's longing for her old routine, her students, the theater, actor gossip. Her dreams were invaded by the screams from the lobsters that Karl tossed into boiling water, and her days disturbed by his taste in music: lieder. Even with him promising not to put it on full blast in the morning, when he did play it, her entire being recoiled. More importantly, once the primary topic of where she would live no longer dominated, she and Karl had less and less to talk about. Yet with her life in a storage unit in Harlem and no place of her own to return to, for the time being she decided this would have to do.

She reached out to the nearest theater company in the area only to be told they were set for the next few plays but were happy to put her name on their roster and call her in for an audition if anything came up. She encountered the same problem with other companies in other parts of the state. And in between long drives to familiarize themselves with the area, touring light-houses, and fishing villages, she continued to scour the internet for an apartment back in the city. At the end of the seventh week her agent called, and she called Julia.

"I'm up for an off-Broadway show. Audition next Tuesday at four," she said trying to play down her excitement—Karl being within earshot. "Can you put up with me for a few days?"

"Of course! That's wonderful. Does Karl know?"

"Of course, Karl knows." Her voice a little louder." "He's happy for me. Anyway, I thought I'd come in on Sunday, spend Monday preparing, getting a wardrobe put together, hair, etc.

etc. Then stay one more night if it's too late to make a train back after the audition. Can you bear it?"

"Definitely, just let me know what time you're arriving. Fingers crossed."

———————

Julia stood at the door to the second bedroom—now converted to an office—and tried to figure out where she would put Esther. If she gave Es the office, then she herself wouldn't have access early in the morning. If she gave Esther the bedroom, then she would have to sleep on the pull-out sofa—fine for a few nights, but there was no telling how long Esther would actually be with her. In the end she decided that she'd take the office. Work over comfort.

On Sunday the doorman called up to announce a delivery from Whole Foods. "But I didn't order anything. Never shop there," she said. She found their prices outrageous.

"It's got your name and apartment number. Should I send him up?"

Esther! Julia thought. Of course! Something she would do. "Please," she said and sure enough, Esther had ordered a variety of organic fruits, a pound of coffee, a box of croissants and what had to be a ridiculously expensive jam with a note, "Help yourself! The croissants are for our breakfast. I promise to get up in time to share. And thank you! Hugs, me"

Maybe that's the other reason she left the theater, Julia thought. Unlike Esther who could stay up most of the night and sleep in till 11, Julia had always risen early. Up at 6, coffee, dressed and made up by 7, checking emails at her desk until 8 and off to work. Even earlier if she had a breakfast meeting. Only on weekends did she manage to stay in bed until 7 or 7:30. She hoped Esther wasn't planning on appearing at midnight.

As it turned out, Esther arrived in time for dinner. "We're going out and it's on me," she announced. "I need to smell New York. The clean air is killing me."

"You've spent enough on breakfast," Julia said. 'Besides, I made a chicken."

"We'll have it tomorrow. Tonight, we're going out! I need to feel the city."

"How did you sleep?" Esther asked as Julia came into the kitchen.

"Since when are you up before me?"

"Need to get to the storage unit to put together an outfit," Esther said. "The role calls for a no-longer viable politician from the Midwest. Well, they can't say I don't look the part about being no-longer viable."

"Stop fishing for a compliment. And as you're the one still having sex, I believe that means you're still viable. You are, aren't you?"

"We are," was all Esther offered up feeling fiercely protective of Karl.

"I probably have things in my closet which would work. Save you the schlepp."

"That's what I miss," Esther said. "No one says, schlepp in Maine."

The audition went well, and Esther was told to come back the following Tuesday. "I think it's between me and one other actress—they won't tell me who. Anyway, going to head back to Maine in the morning. Let you get a good night sleep in your own bed. First thing tomorrow, train to Boston, bus to Portland where Karl will pick me up. His place not too long a drive from there."

What she left out was how displaced she felt floating between Julia's apartment in New York and Karl's cabin in Maine. How she wanted her own, her anchor, her home, so she could safely leap off into space.

At first it had been fun for Julia to prep Esther for the audition, listening to her doing speech exercises, even doing them with her. But slowly painful old feelings rose up. Emotions that had taken years of therapy to quell. Years during which she couldn't set foot in a theater as she worked to overcome the loss of her dream. Hours confronting her need to stand on the stage with a spotlight focused on her in order to receive the attention she craved. The contrast with Esther now more apparent than ever. Ether just loved the process itself. The development of a character. The interaction with other actors. Maybe that's why she hadn't been more successful. She didn't need all eyes on her. Julia feared that if Esther stayed with her too long, Julia would be catapulted back to that very dark time.

Well, at least for now, she was back in her own bed, though she considered getting a new mattress for the sofa if Esther's visits became more frequent. The cheaper model she'd bought originally, killing her back.

In spite of knowing better—being incredibly superstitious like most actors—Esther began checking out AirB&Bs as well as cheap hotels in the city, especially those in or near the theater district. She figured that with the money she'd received for the apartment, along with what she'd be earning, she could manage. Maybe even pull her things out of storage. Yes, it would mean that she wouldn't see Karl for the run of the show, but he could always come into town on the night they were dark.

She returned to Julia's the night before the call-back. This time they ate in. No bottle of wine. Just reading lines. A good night's sleep. A workout at Julia's gym in the morning, and off to the theater. The verdict to come the following morning.

"I didn't get it," she told Julia as she put down the phone. "And I gave a damn good reading. Not just good. Great! You could have heard a pin drop."

"I'm so sorry, Julia said, "putting her arms around her. "Truly sorry. What are you going to do now?"

"Have no idea." And she didn't. Had been here before, but this rejection felt far more consequential.

"You can stay here while you figure it out," Julia said.

"No, I need to get up to Karl. Talk things out with him. I can't just say I'm not coming back over the phone."

"Then you're not going to stay with him?"

"I don't know, damnit! Sorry, but I keep thinking it's my fault. I shouldn't have checked out those AirB&Bs, allowed myself to think I had the part. I jinxed it."

"Don't be a crazy actor!"

Esther felt she'd been slapped. Must have shown it because Julia quickly added, "I didn't mean that."

"You really don't like actors, do you? All that therapy of yours, what? Made you think you had cured yourself of some mental illness by giving up the stage? Well, let me tell you, we might be nuts, but so are the people in your business. Just a different kind of nuts." It was getting out of hand.

"You're right," Julia said, her voice subdued. "I'm so sorry. Listen, the apartment is yours whenever you need it. I'm here if you need me."

Esther could feel her nerve endings relax. She did have an anchor here. "Thank you," she said, grateful. "Let me go back and talk to Karl. Love you."

"Love you too."

The following week Julia replaced her sofa with one deep enough to allow herself a good night's sleep without having to remove pull it open. She also bought a new set of sheets, two new pillows, cleared out two drawers in the bedroom and made room in her closet for Esther to hang her clothes. She had no doubt Esther would be back. Esther's affairs never having lasted more than six months.

"I found an apartment!" Esther said in a monotone.

Julia assumed she was trying to sound matter of fact so as not to hurt Karl lest he be listening.

"Where?" Julia asked, strangely disappointed that her preparations had been for naught.

"Washington Heights. A one-bedroom. The only stairs I'll have to contend with are the subway's. Between social security, teaching Pilates, and royalties from the cameo on Law and Order, I should be fine."

"How's Karl taking it?"

"He'll be okay, I think." And then in almost a whisper. "I'm sure there are plenty of widows in Maine who would welcome a widower into their lives."

Esther sensed that Karl had known from the beginning that she was a bridge between the past and his future. Still, for the next few weeks until the apartment became available, they both acted as if their being together was forever. The only difference, the sex became more intense as the end loomed. Karl came down to help move her belongings from the storage unit into the new apartment. No, it wasn't close to the theater district. But one subway ride put her there if an audition or a go-see came up. She contacted her old students and they agreed to pay a bit more so she could rent a studio by the hour on West 36th Street for classes. She was back!

She and Julia went back to their once a month get togethers, Esther travelling down on the number 1 train, then walking or bussing across town to Julia's. They would curl up on the new sofa and, depending on the time of day, either indulge in tea, coffee and pastries or break open a bottle of wine. If it got too late, Julia would insist on sending Esther home in an Uber or make her stay overnight convincing her with, "Have to use the new sheets and sofa or why did I spend all that money?"

"So, what's new?" one of them would ask as they would settle in.

"You first," the other would reply.

Most times Esther would relay a story about a play she'd seen, one that she should have been cast in. Or Julia relayed the latest family saga. All familiar until the day Julia announced she was quitting her job, retiring. "I've had it. We've been invaded by teeny boppers."

Esther was as shocked by Julia's decision as by her own reaction of feeling dislodged. "But you've loved your work. Seemed to get so much satisfaction from it. What will you do?"

"I don't know. Travel. Take classes. Volunteer. . . I'll figure it out. It's time, Es."

Esther couldn't imagine not working, but then work for her had always been sporadic, veering off to the side then back again.

As if reading her thoughts Julia asked if she'd ever consider retiring. "Only when my mind no longer could retain the lines, or my body gives out. Besides old actors will always be needed to play the grandmother or a senile old biddy. I might finally be continually employed."

A faint smile played around Julia's lips. "Ever thought what our lives would have been like if we had possessed just a bit of the other?"

"I don't know. What part of me would you have wanted, Julia? Now really?"

Who's Counting

"I was thinking. How many times do you think we've actually seen each other?"

"You mean physically been together? I don't know. Not many. I'd guess about 16 or 17. Not including that week at the writer's workshop. But then we didn't actually talk to each other until the very last day."

"So how about we count that as one?"

"Well, then the second would have had to have been when the group reconvened at my house."

"God, I loved that story of yours. All those women spontaneously combusting all over New Jersey. Who knew that's what you yourself were doing—figuratively of course. Did we have one or two more workshop reunions after that?"

"I think only one. We're up to three."

"So much for continuing as a group. No matter, by then we had already started chatting on the phone. I think I reached out to you first. Too few writers in my life and I couldn't get over your story."

"Well, I had no confidantes in mine and clearly needed one. I think that's when I invited you out to my place."

"Introduced me to the Port Authority along with your kids. As I remember James was away."

"For a change. That makes four."

"Then the fifth would have been when I joined the two of you and another couple for dinner in the city."

"The Hashburns!"

"Right. James certainly not what I expected."

"Trust me. Turned out not to have been what I'd expected either."

"Clever. I know I came out to Montclair for your reading, six."

"And James and I came in with guacamole for your 65th, seven."

The best ever! The guacamole not the birthday."

"Did I come in with Ken before or after the divorce?"

"During, eight. Remember I called him your exit man as he was going to help you get out the door."

"I know I went with you to the theater twice. Once downtown. Once on Broadway. But I can't tell you what we saw, ten.

"There was that lunch and the walk on the Highline two summers ago, eleven."

"And before that you were out here for my 60th, twelve."

"Oh, and you came in for my 80th which *was* the best ever. We're getting up there, thirteen."

"I also came in for your play reading. No, wait! Both readings. So, fifteen."

"Then there was drinks with what's his name. The one you brought in for my approval, sixteen."

"Don. And we're forgetting the day you came out to help me hang pictures in the new apartment, seventeen."

"Add in the two times I got together with you and Mark—I can't get over how you two mesh—anyway, so maybe nineteen times in nineteen years give or take?"

"Crazy. You know if we were born in a different time, we would have been writing our innermost thoughts to each other instead of spilling them out on the phone. Could have made for a damn good book."

"Not sure we'd want anyone reading it even if we were long gone."

"Probably not."

They both put down their phones. They'd talk again later in the day. They always did.

What Would I Do Without You?

"You wouldn't believe how willing some women are. You walk in the door and they're ready to skip all the get to know you's, and hop straight into bed."

Her moment of solitude obviously over, Ruth rose from her seat by the window in the breakfast nook, took her mug and phone to the counter—hitting speaker—and began setting up Jim's tray. "So, who was she last night?"

"Sue Grenfield. Lives in Long Island. Nice enough, but too long a trip. Once was enough."

"And tonight? Or are you going to give yourself a night off?" Ruth knew she was living vicariously. But at 57, better than not living at all. Besides, she deserved whatever pleasure she could get no matter how she got it, and Ed's calls gave her pleasure whatever hour they came in. "Maybe you could stay home? Spend an evening with the kids?" Her brother might think he had the stamina of a twenty-year-old but, even at 54, performing nightly was a little insane. Bad enough the kids had lost their mother; they didn't need their father dying in some stranger's bed.

"C'mon, Ruth. I'm home for the kids' dinner almost every night. With them all weekend. So, relax. Anyway, staying in this evening. Next subject! How's Jim this morning?"

"Same." She ladled the oatmeal into Jim's bowl, then set it on the tray along with his spoon—the thick handle allowing him to feed himself, at least for now.

"Wish you'd get more help."

"Sorry, gotta go. Jim's breakfast is ready. Love you." As much as she loved his calls, she could do without Ed joining the chorus of well-intentioned buttinskies. She was more than capable of taking care of her husband. Enough she had an aide come every morning to wash him, get him dressed—anything to preserve what little dignity he had left. The rest she could do herself, thank you very much. She looked at the clock. 7:30. Right on schedule. She left the kitchen and headed to what was once their den.

"Get that smile on! Breakfast is here!" An unnecessary command. It was rare Jim didn't smile whenever he saw her.

"Wa-s that E-d on the phone?" His speech slow, dragged out.

"He bedded another one."

Jim laughed—or what went for a laugh nowadays. Her eyes instinctively went to the bag hanging off the side of the bed even though she'd already emptied it earlier. She set his breakfast down on the tray table, raised the bed, fixed the pillows behind his head, positioning the food in front of him. "This one lives in Long Island. Said it was too far to travel to see her again."

"Serv-ic-ing the Met-ro-pol-it-an a-re-a, huh?"

"That's what he seems to be doing," she said closing his hand around the spoon. "Need any more help, luv?"

"All set. You go! Sho—wer."

"Be back in a few."

Through the monitor she could hear the spoon hitting the side of the bowl. It was okay. He needed to do for himself whatever he could for as long as he could. She kept her showers short and decisive. Rinse, soap, rinse again and out. Longer than that her mind went to places she didn't want it to go. She was drying off when she heard the downstairs door open and the aide announce he'd arrived.

"I'm upstairs, Paul," she called down. "He's all yours." She ran the comb through her hair. Estelle would have said it needed color. "Haven't had time," she said aloud as if Estelle could still hear her. "And you needn't have worried about him marrying the first woman he met." With that she ran a red lipstick over her lips and headed to the closet.

The one saving grace about having to take care of Jim was that at the end of the day she was so exhausted she rarely craved sex. Not the way she did the first year of his illness when they could still try various forms of intimacy until the failures depressed them both and it was better she take care of herself in the shower or expend her energy on a tennis court. Enough! She threw on a pair of navy slacks and a white shirt, made the bed, then headed downstairs just as Paul was finishing. Thankfully, she didn't find him attractive unlike the first aide whom she'd dreamed about for weeks—caretaking-in-tandem breeding far too much intimacy.

"All done?" she asked.

"In his chair and ready to go. You sure you don't want me to take him out?"

"No, I'm fine, thanks. See you tomorrow."

"Yes ma'am."

Jim smiled at her from the wheelchair. "Paul fix-ed me up."

"So I see. All dressed and looking quite handsome, I must say."

"And goo-d morn-ing a-gain to you."

She should be grateful for his compliancy, but there were times she wanted him to scream, to rant, to rave, but that was not his way. He had kept his grief muted even when their Robbie died.

Oh, the tears had flowed, but he never ranted. He'd left that to her.

The phone rang again. She picked up the receiver next to Jim's bed automatically touching Robbie's picture on the nightstand.

"Me again. Guess who just called?"

"Who?"

"Guess."

She gave Jim a look of mock frustration. "Ed, really! Who?"

"Marilyn Bloom. Wants to fix me up. Says she's been holding back until enough time passed. Can you believe?"

Ruth positioned the phone so Jim could listen in. "Well, she did well the first time. So, are you going to call?" Not that Ruth thought for a minute Ed would pass up a new name. Especially one coming from Estelle's high school friend.

"Do you think Marilyn told her she'd fixed Estelle and me up?"

"And if she did?"

"Don't want to raise any hopes. Anyway, the only thing Marilyn would tell me is that she's a widow."

"Well, knowing Marilyn, she must have had a good reason to hold off until now. And anyway, widows are supposed to do well with widowers."

"Okay. But I'll blame you if it's a lousy evening."

"Good-bye Ed." She waited for Jim to get his hands onto the controls. "Ready?" When Jim nodded, they headed into the kitchen.

A few minutes later, the phone rang again. "Yes?"

"She can't see me for a whole week and only wants to meet for a drink."

"Obviously, she's not desperate. What's her name?"

"Vera. Vera Teller."

"Don't know her. So, did you make a date?"

"Yeah, for next Friday—a week from tomorrow."

"I'll be interested to hear. Talk later." And with that she hung up, reheated her coffee, moved Jim to be closer to the counter, steeled herself and dialed Estelle's parents. "How are you two today?" she asked, knowing full well what was coming.

"You of all people should know. Nothing worse than losing a child, is there? But then you have two more."

Ruth did everything she could to keep herself from letting out a scream. Yes, she had two girls. Was grateful for them. Grateful that both were living their own lives. Andrea and her husband teaching at the American Academy in Rome. Susie head of nursing upstate—on call if needed. Both checking in weekly.

But that didn't minimize Robbie's absence. She could feel Jim's eyes trying to calm her as he always did. She took a deep breath. "Why don't you two plan a trip," she said. "A cruise? Maybe widen your circle?"

And as if on cue Estelle's mom, her voice wary, asked, "So is he seeing anyone special?"

"Not that I know of."

"Good. Clearly way too soon."

"It's been three years, Jean. He's a father alone."

"Too soon."

And knowing the tears were about to start, Ruth extricated herself from the conversation using Jim calling her as an excuse. "They would prefer Ed would be alone forever!" she hissed as she slammed down the phone. "I wish to hell I hadn't promised Estelle I'd take care of them. At some point they are going to have to stop wallowing in their grief. They could be reaching out to their grandchildren, for God's sake."

"Est-elle w-as their li-fe. Their on-ly chi-ld."

"Let's not go there, okay?" She wiped off the counter, tossed the dishes into the dishwasher, and clapped her hands together. "Okay. Enough! What would you like to do today?"

"U-p to you."

"Then a shop. Get whatever we need for the weekend. How's that?"

He was still able, with her help of course, to maneuver himself out of the wheelchair into the car. She'd long ago figured out how to wheel Jim through the Supermarket, a basket on his lap, flipping most of whatever they needed into it as if she was on a basketball court, then emptying the contents into the cart that she'd left at the manager's station—repeating the routine until all items were amassed. The entire procedure carried out with a smile on her face, often even humming a tune. And no, it was not martyrdom, no matter what others thought. She just didn't want any looks of pity for both of them.

She'd been fighting sleep—the TV on—when Ed rang.

"What do you think of The Renaissance as a place to go for a drink?"

"Just make a reservation. It's Friday night and you might want to extend it to dinner."

"Yeah, though if she's true to form, we'll probably stay in."

"Very funny." He really was a child. "Good night, Ed."

Ed's calls had begun when Estelle first went into the hospital. Ed desperate for guidance regarding the kids, or needing to discuss what a doctor had said, or simply solace. Before Ed it was Estelle on the phone. "Just checking up on your two," she'd say, and Ruth would respond with "We're fine." Even though they weren't. Would never be. The loss of their only son forever haunting. They were okay, but they certainly weren't fine.

"So, how did it go?" Ruth asked.

"Good, I think."

"Continue."

"She has three kids!"

"And you have two, so?"

"That would make five!"

"I can count."

"She also works!"

"Good for her. At what?"

"Guidance counselor. She was studying to be a shrink but changed her mind when her first kid was born."

"Ed, did you have a good time?"

"She asks a lot of questions."

"Such as?"

"How my kids are doing. How Estelle died. Was our marriage a good one."

"She's probably trying to see if you're marriage material."

"Not ready."

"How long since her husband passed?"

"Three years."

"Like you. Are you going to see her again?"

"Said I'd call."

"Well, I think you should."

Definitely, it was time he found someone. The kids needed a mother figure though one with three competing siblings might not be the best choice. Still, Marilyn had been spot-on the first time, so there had to be a reason she saved Vera for now. Not that Estelle could be replaced. She couldn't be. Not for Ed, the kids, or herself. But it would be nice to have a someone to share the load, perhaps even a confidante. She certainly had been closer to Estelle than even her own sister. Alice had never shared. Couldn't. All wrapped up in herself. No, her closest sibling had always been Ed, brought all the closer because she and Estelle had been drawn to each other from day one.

"Have a problem," Ed said one morning.

"The kids okay?"

"Yeah, yeah, with Vera."

"What?

"She expects me not to see anyone else now that we're sleeping together."

"Well, that's understandable." Ed had already let on a few weeks back that the 'dirty deed' was done—the same words he'd used when in his last year at High School he'd informed her he was no longer a virgin.

"I'd expect the same. So, when am I going to meet her?"

"C'mon. Bringing her over to you means I'm signaling a commitment and I'm not ready to take on a woman with three kids."

"For heaven's sake, Ed. You obviously like her. And whether or not you think you're not ready to commit, you seem to be only seeing her. Besides, you introduced us to what's her name—Mary. And you extricated yourself from that. Look, how about you drop by for drinks one night. We'll keep it very casual."

". . . I'll think about it."

"Good."

"Why a-re you pu-shing it?" Jim asked as soon as she hung up.

"Because I'd like to meet her."

"She's no-t go-ing to be E-st-elle."

Jim's body may no longer function, but his mind was as spot on as ever.

"I just think if she's the one then I want her to know us. See us as family. Not splinter him and the children off as often happens."

Ruth was more than pleasantly surprised, if not relieved, when she got a call from Vera inviting Jim and her to dinner. "That's so nice of you, Vera. We'd be delighted though you know, it might be easier if you came here, what with Jim's wheelchair and all." But Vera said that her house's interior was wheelchair accessible and Ed could easily lift him up the few stairs at the entrance.

Ruth had to laugh at herself as to how long it took for her to decide what to wear. Ridiculous really. She wasn't one for dressing up. Not that her closet held that many choices. Besides, she couldn't imagine a guidance counselor's wardrobe being any fancier than hers. No, she would dress as she always did. A nice pair of slacks, a sweater with a scarf to spruce things up, and one nice piece of jewelry. The same as Estelle would have worn if she were alive. How often had they collapsed in laughter when they would meet up and find themselves in matching outfits.

There was no mirror moment when Vera opened the door clothed in a filmy black dress, high heels, and long silver earrings. Extremely thin, almost fragile in appearance, she was so unlike Estelle who had been of average height and athletically built. What had happened to men going for the same type over and over, Ruth wondered. No matter, she consoled herself, she was as dressed as she needed to be for a relaxed get-to-know-you dinner.

"It's so good to finally meet you, Ruth," Vera's voice, as on the phone, soft, soothing. "I love that he has a sister with whom he is so close."

"And I am pleased to meet you as well," Ruth smiled.

"You ha-ve a bea-u-tiful ho-me," Jim offered.

"Thank you, Jim. We were only here a year before Jacob, my husband, died. So much left undone. Ed has been a Godsend, spending hours fixing up the place. Fixed all the shutters. I was going to hire someone, but Ed insisted he do it. And he did. All of them."

A chill went through Ruth. Ed hadn't said a word. Not one. With all the other details he'd offered, he'd omitted the most telling of how involved he actually was.

"We go-t stu-ff you cou-ld fi-x at ho-me Ed, i-f you want."

Everyone laughed though Ruth's came out like a loud guffaw. The evening progressed with Ed playing bartender even though there was no need. Jim could no longer drink, and Ruth had lost her taste for alcohol in the process. Vera made it clear that Ruth was not allowed to help in any way dashing Ruth's fantasy of the two women chatting away as they stacked the dishes in the dishwasher. Only Ed had kitchen privileges—something he took to all too willingly. It wasn't until the end of the evening when Vera suggested she and Ruth get together, "just us gals" that Ruth's hopes revived. "Would love that," she said. "And as you're the one with three kids and a job, you say when. Jim's quite good about taking care of himself for a few hours."

They settled on the following Sunday afternoon. Vera's kids would be at their grandparents and at Vera's suggestion Ed would bring his kids over to keep Jim company.

"She'll fit in well, don't you think?" Ruth asked Jim on their way home.

"Fi-t in-to wha-t?"

"The family."

"Who-se?"

"Ours of course. C'mon. You know what I mean. She'll be a fine addition."

"She ha-s fam-il-y of her o-wn."

"I know, but so did Estelle."

"E-ste-lle ha-d no sib-lings. Diff-rant."

Ruth shook off the thought. Besides, it was Vera who had reached out to her, so clearly, she too was looking for someone to attach herself to in the family.

The phone rang first thing it the morning. "Well, what do you think?"

"Clearly you're smitten."

"Still have doubts about taking on three more kids."

"Well, I think you can do it. Besides you'd be sharing them. How about I give you a thumbs up or down after next Sunday? Though what I say shouldn't matter."

Ruth's week was full. An unexpected emergency room visit after Alice crashed her car into a telephone pole then had to be checked into rehab—for how long no one knew. The usual trip to Jim's doctor—thankfully, things were status quo, and a surprise visit from Susie on her way to a conference. Before she knew it, Sunday had arrived.

Ruth picked Vera up at her house. This time Vera wore slacks, but it was the poncho fringed top and long dangling earrings that brought Estelle's favorite expression, 'artsy fartsy', to mind.

"What a lovely idea, going to The Inn," Vera said as she climbed into Ruth's car.

"Just thought it would give us the chance to sip tea and chat."

"To chat or give me the third degree? Ed says if you don't approve, I'm out. I like to think he was joking, but I can't be sure."

"Of course, he was joking. Anyway, I expect it's going to be more the other way around. That I'll be in the hot seat answering questions."

"Well, I do have questions. Mostly about the kids."

"What about them?" her guard up.

"Just concerned. I gather there were long periods when they were without their mom."

"Estelle did the best she could!" Ruth hadn't meant to sound so defensive, but she'd be damned if whoever followed her would be allowed to voice a negative thought. "Trust me, no matter how sick, Estelle managed to talk with them daily." All right, so that was an exaggeration, but not by much.

"I didn't mean to imply she hadn't." Vera said. "Just that I can't imagine what that must have been like for the children and what effect it had. All five kids have suffered. With Jacob, he was here one day and gone the next. It took a long time for all of us to get over the shock. Not sure my kids are to this day."

Somewhat mollified, Ruth went on, "Estelle was a part of all our lives as long as she could be. She even woke from a coma to call me on the anniversary of our Robbie's passing."

"I am so sorry about your son. I can't imagine."

Ruth stopped herself from saying 'no you can't'. "Do you play tennis?" she asked.

"Used to but hurt my shoulder so that put an end to it. I gather you're an avid player."

"Keeps me alive. Estelle and I played all the time until she got ill." She had to stop bringing up Estelle.

"Losing a son and a best friend had to be awful. And please, Ruth, understand I am in no way trying to replace Estelle. I couldn't just as Ed couldn't replace Jacob. But I'd love to know more about the family dynamic. And the children's relationships with their grandparents. I certainly would want to keep as much in place as possible if—and it's a big if as he hasn't asked me yet—we marry."

They spent most of the afternoon with Ruth filling Vera in about what she would be up against as far as Estelle's parents were concerned, Ed's loyalty to them, and about his not being much of a disciplinarian having left the hard stuff to Estelle. Ruth felt it her duty to make sure nothing was sugar coated so that if they did decide to marry, there'd be no surprises. Vera didn't seem daunted. As a matter of fact, Ruth got the impression Vera was eager to take on the challenge. Yes, Ruth would definitely give her stamp of approval. She would go to bed that night with a sense of calm knowing there'd be more questions to come and that she'd be the one Vera would turn to.

"So, should I run for the hills?" Ed asked later in the day.

"We had a lovely time and I think you'd be crazy not to marry her. She is exactly what you need."

———————————

Ruth threw the engagement party. She and Vera worked together on the list as to whom to invite. The friends were easy. As were siblings. Then they tackled the grandparents.

"There's no problem on our side," Ruth said. "As you know, Ed and my parents, are long gone. Jim's wouldn't expect to be invited, though it might be nice to do so. It's Estelle's parents I worry about."

"Same with Jacob's. Of course, my mom will be there. But why don't you talk to Estelle's and I'll talk to Jacob's. Explain how we want to keep the families intact on both sides. Then see if they even want to get an invitation."

Much to Ruth's surprise, Estelle's parents decided to attend though not until the last minute. Even more surprising, they ended up choosing to sit with Jacob's parents in what Ruth would later label, 'the Mourner's Corner.' Still, if not a joyous event, it did allow everyone to get their bearings. Ed's oldest,

Evie, even made a toast holding up her glass of ginger ale, saying how she hoped her dad would be as happy with Vera as he was with her mother. Not to be outdone, Vera's Jake got up and said he knew his Dad was up in heaven watching. Then Susie, who had come down for the party, tried to take the edge off with a wish that Ed and Vera continue to love each other as much as her own mom and dad did.

She had just finished bringing Jim his breakfast when Ed called.

"We've decided to have the wedding at City Hall."

"Really?" He'd already informed her that they were going to move into Vera's home, something Ruth did not think the wisest of ideas believing that Vera's kids could treat Ed's like intruders.

"Vera feels that by keeping it low key, it will be easier on the kids."

"Well, if that's what you want, of course we'll be there . . . Ed?"

"Vera wants to keep it just the immediate family. You know, us and the kids. If she invites you, she'll have to invite the other aunts and uncles, and it becomes a big thing. You understand, right?"

Ruth barely managed to choke out an, "Of course."

"Don't get me wrong. I would love for you to be there, Ruth. But it does make sense when you think about it, right?"

When they hung up, Ruth couldn't move.

"Wha-t's wr-ong?"

She just nodded her head.

"So-me-thi-ng i-s."

Then, as if she were spitting teeth that had just been knocked out, "They're going to City Hall for the wedding. We're not invited."

Jim tried to calm her down. To get her to see the quandary Vera and Ed were in. "They w-ould ha-ve to in-vi-te ev-ery-one." But there was no way he could close the wound that had just been inflicted.

Over time, Ed's calls came with far less frequency. Ruth even got to a place where she stopped expecting them, was almost surprised when the phone rang, and he was on the other end.

"Hey, Ruth! Any idea of what I should get Vera for her birth-day?"

"Are you planning something special?"

"No, she's made it clear she wants to be at home with the children. I'll order take out and a cake that way she won't have to cook."

"Well, she seems to like unusual jewelry. Do you want me to look around? See what I can find?"

"What would I do without you? Thanks!"

Ruth made an outing of it. She took Jim to the Arts and Crafts center in the next town, pushing his wheelchair from stand to stand until she found a pendant hammered in silver with a black stone almost like an eye. She put it on hold, then called Ed telling him to check it out.

"Well, did she like it?" Ruth asked a week later.

"Said she did."

"But?"

"When I told her you'd helped me find it, she got upset. Said I should at least have gone with you."

"Why did you tell her? And you did pick it up."

"I-t's be-tween the-m," Jim said after she repeated what had occurred. "Leave i-t alone."

"But I always picked out his gifts for Estelle."

"Lee-ve it."

It was the next call that did Ruth in. Ed's voice sheepish. Apologetic.

"It's Evie's choice, Ruth."

"Evie's or Vera's?" the rage welling up. "I've been a part of your kids' lives since before Estelle got ill," she seethed. "And once she did, it was I who hosted every damn birthday. Saw to it they were mothered as much as mine if not more. And now I'm excluded? Her sixteenth?"

"It's what she wanted. Only kids. No adults."

"You'll be there, right?"

"Of course, but in another room. As chaperones. Hey, you were the one who said Vera was what I and the kids needed. You can take Evie out to celebrate whenever you want."

"Well, thank you for allowing me to see my niece. She's still my niece, isn't she?"

"Of course. Just as you are my sister. But you're not my mother, Ruth. Nor the kids. That's Vera's job now. And she's trying hard to fill that role."

Ruth could hardly say goodbye or even turn off the phone—her entire being drained of energy. She just stood there rocking back and forth, her arms wrapped around her body. She needed Jim to hold her, to put salve on the wound. But that would no long be possible—the latest turn in his condition confining him to bed.

She watched him make the effort to turn his head towards her as she entered.

"Wha-t's wro-ng?" he said. Concern contorted on his face.

"Nothing," she lied desperately trying to smile.

"So-mething. Is it me?"

"No, of course not!"

"Ru-th-ie, pl-ease," he rasped. "Don't wo-rry. It'll be o-kay. Ed'll loo-k aft-er you when I'm gone. Ju-st like you've always loo-ked aft-er him."

Saying Goodbye

"How long have I known you?"

"53 years."

"Really? That long?"

"That long."

"And how old are you?"

"Seventy-six."

"Impossible."

Karen wondered how long she could keep this up. This blip of conversation repeated over and over—the same whether she visits or phones. She waited, and sure enough right on cue, Barbara made her demand.

"Tell me something new!"

Karen repeated what she'd said moments before. "John passed away."

"He lives in California, yes?"

"Lived. He's dead."

"Oh, is he?"

How this bit of trivia as to where John lived had settled in Barbara's brain bewildered Karen. It couldn't even be classified under long-term memory. Karen herself couldn't remember when John had left the East Coast. When he'd remarried. Started a new life. Simply that in the past few years he called only on her birthday rather than when he was feeling in need of a Karen fix. Yet John and California had lodged in Barbara's brain like a crumb between two teeth. Karen rose from her hard-backed chair at the foot of Barbara's bed—a brown metal rented hospital contraption with raised crib-like sides.

"Are you leaving?" Barbara asked, her mouth spread in a wide partially toothless grin. Karen found Barbara's sweetness unnerving. So different from the sharp edge that had defined her. The person Karen had written about in article after article, monogram after monogram, not to mention the complete biography the publisher was waiting for Karen to finish.

"Just going to walk around a bit. Stretch my legs. I'll be back," Karen said knowing that when she returned the entire scenario would repeat itself verbatim. But she needed a break. She walked down the hall to the living room passing Barbara's paintings stacked up one against the other wherever space existed. "There will come a day when I'll stop making art," Barbara had announced somewhere in her mid-70's. Karen had roared when she'd said it. "Oh sure, like you ever would stop. You'll probably drop dead in your studio at the ripe young age of 117." But Barbara did indeed stop. Three years ago. Not only stopped but had her studio cleared out the day after her 90th birthday.

That morning Karen had decided to surprise Barbara and pop into the studio with her favorite pastries 'to start the next decade with sweets' only to arrive in time to witness a succession of young artists descend like scavengers. They were carrying off tools, camera equipment, tubes of paints—whether used or not—sacks of plaster, rolls of canvas, stretchers of all sizes, whatever they could lay their hands on, without even a "Thank you" or a "May I?" They seemed to know exactly what to take uttering just an "Excuse me ma'am" as they raced passed Karen pressed against the wall lest she be trampled upon. "What's happening?" she'd cried. But Barbara—her back turned to the goings on—ignored her. Unable to fathom the scene, Karen had grabbed the arm of a tall lanky long-haired boy, outfitted in the obligatory paint splattered jeans, torn denim jacket with more paint stains over a dingy T who looked like he hadn't eaten in weeks, and demanded an explanation. "Hey, I'm just following her orders," he'd muttered as he pushed his overflowing cart out of Karen's reach and his arm out of her grasp. "She" his head tilted towards where Barbara stood, "set this up."

Not until the studio was laid bare of all but Barbara's pieces in various stages of completion, did she turn around, her eyes straight ahead, and stride across the loft. "I didn't want it all to end up in the trash," her voice almost lifeless. Then, "Damn, they could have taken these," referring to the coffee pot and mugs. "I have so many at home."

Karen's whole being gasped for air "I don't understand. You planned this?"

"Told them they could each take whatever they needed, just to get it over with fast."

Karen's words flew out of her. "Overnight you decided to empty out your studio? Why didn't you say something? Does Ellie know? Did you tell her you were going to do this?"

Only then did Barbara's pent-up emotions spew forth flinging themselves at Karen. "My daughter has enough on her plate! And you, you'd try to keep me working because you wouldn't want to end your book on a downer. Wouldn't want to write that I lost the ability to produce art. Wouldn't have that 'She produced art until her last breath' dramatic ending. You've seen my handshake. Did you say anything? No. Pretended it doesn't exist. How the fucking hell do you think I can draw nevertheless paint with a shaking arm? How?"

Yes, Karen had noticed Barbara's shaky hand whenever she picked up a cup of coffee, but she'd also seen how fast she brought the other one up to steady it. "You appeared to want to hide the tremors," Karen said, her voice trembling. "So, I remained mute. And as far as the book goes, damnit Barbara, I haven't spent all these years writing about you and your work as you presented it to me to suddenly want to control the story."

"A leech," Barbara had mumbled.

"What? What did you say?"

"You're a leech," Barbara's voice now a razor thin scream. "You think you're a writer. You're not a writer. If it weren't for me, you wouldn't have been able to string two words together. They're all my thoughts. My ideas. Mine! All mine." Then, just as fast as Barbara's screaming had started, it stopped, and her voice became almost childlike in its innocence, "Do you want a cup of coffee?" she said. "You take it black, don't you?" and then with gleeful delight, "Oh, look, you brought goodies."

Karen could neither race to the door nor reach for the coffee Barbara held out to her. The confluence of the suddenly sterile studio, Barbara's venomous rage, followed by her solicitousness as if nothing had transpired, shackled Karen in place. Had she just witnessed the first signs of dementia? Had there been others and she'd either missed them or turned a blind eye? She knew she should call Ellie. Tell her she needed to come to NY. But what would she say? That Barbara had proclaimed her to be a fraud then offered coffee? Karen couldn't believe the hurt she felt and how, in a split-second, Barbara had reopened all of Karen's self-doubts. Doubts about not being original. About not really being a writer. Doubts that Barbara herself had squelched many times starting way back after an evening—maybe two years into their knowing each other—when Karen, having consumed far too much wine, had confessed her fears. "Oh, for

God's sake," Barbara had admonished. "You're a damn good writer and you know it. Everyone has doubts. Get over it." A sentiment she'd repeat whenever Karen got down on herself. Had all Barbara's words of encouragement simply been a way to create her own personal scribe? To make sure her thoughts were set down for posterity? Karen felt slashed. Her soul cut by hundreds of glass shards each etched with the word 'leech.' It took all her strength to accept the coffee, take Barbara home and call Ellie. Only later did she remember the pastries left on the counter.

Things spiraled downward after that. First came an untreated bout of pneumonia with Barbara's new doctor—her old one retired—sending Barb by herself to a street clinic rather than an ER. Then a urinary infection that produced hallucinations causing the dementia to catapult forward at lightning speed. "I begged her to go to a hospital," Karen had told Ellie. "Begged her." She did not mention the guilt she felt at not having gone across town and dragged Barbara herself. But being with Barbara had gotten too difficult. And Karen, stung by the leech remark, had convinced herself it would be better to stay away.

A few days after the studio's cleaning out, Barbara's dealer had come by and chosen the pieces she thought would sell; the rest, including the unfinished canvases, went to Barbara's home. Within a week there was nothing left to do but sweep and let the realtor do her job. The swiftness had caught Karen off-guard. Yes, she had expected the day would come when the studio would be emptied, and the door closed. But she'd thought it would occur after Barbara was gone, after she and Ellie had spent weeks if not months crying and laughing together as they sorted through the studio's contents, shared memories and stories until they came to terms with the end of a life. But that was then, and this is where they were now.

Karen began to rifle through the paintings against the wall, pulling the frames forward, glancing down. Unnecessary. She knew them all. So many days spent composing words that would capture their essence. Now she worried whether she'd find enough words to finish the book. The computer's thesaurus doing so much of her brain's work in the last few months. The doctor's pronouncement never far from her thoughts.

"Ms. Winfred,"

"Karen. Please."

"Karen. You've had what we refer to as a TIA. A mini-stroke."

She knew what a TIA was. Had watched what a series of them had done to her mother. The horrors they'd inflicted on her brain. "My words...." She mumbled. Half a question, half a plea.

"Everyone's different. It depends what part of the brain is affected."

But Karen's words had been affected. She'd find herself staring at the computer screen while she reached back into her brain desperately searching for a word that used to easily find its way to her fingertips. And now the last chapter of The Life and Works of Barbara G. Kaplan as compiled by Karen Winfred remained unwritten. Waiting. She heard Barbara calling out for the aide and rushed back to the room.

"What are you doing here?" Barbara asked a smile of delight crossing her hollowed out face.

"I came to visit. Told Dee she could go shopping while I'm here."

"And why does she need to shop?"

"For food."

"Oh. . . How long have I known you?"

She wanted to say, "too long," but bit her tongue. Karen watched as Barbara's eyes fixated on the piece across from her bed. A screaming man's head emerging from the canvas. What Karen described in Chapter four as 'the origin of the vortex to follow.' Not that it swirled. No, it extended out into the room. A sculpted head that pulled the canvas off the stretcher. One of Barbara's early attempts at combining two mediums. Why this was what Barbara had chosen to put on the wall so it would be the first thing she saw in the morning and the last at night did not make sense to Karen until in one of those rare moments of lucidity Barbara explained, "It reminds me of how a failed canvas, instead of pulling me further into a creative funk, could fill me with so much rage, I'd be ready to begin again." Then the moment ended, and Barbara drifted off into her fog of dementia. "I think I'll go to the studio tomorrow. What do you think of that?" she said, and Karen had left the room to cry uncontrollably from the pain of having her friend back for a moment then losing her again.

Dee returned and Karen retreated to the living room where her laptop sat opened on the coffee table— a guilt-inducing reminder that the final pages were waiting for Barbara to pass. Karen dreaded Barbara's will to live as much as she dreaded her death. A feeling not shared by Karen's publisher or agent. They were ghouls. "Just write the last chapter as if she were already gone," they kept telling her. "We can add the exact date of her death as we get closer to the publishing date. Just like an obit. Those writers write them years in advance." She'd tried. Written it in her head over and over. Standing in the shower. Walking down the street. Lying in bed. The chapter to be a personal reflection starting with their first meeting.

"The gallery assigned you?"

"Just for the pamphlet. If you could give me a quote? Something about your work. And review the bio. If you would."

"Hate the way most writers write about art. A bunch of crap if you ask me."

"A quote?"

"Art is for the eye aimed at the heart. If it doesn't move you, it's not art."

"And the bio?"

"Cut out the lines about my being a woman artist. I'm an artist. Finished."

"Got it. Thanks."

But the ending. . .to put that down meant she'd be killing off her friend and her friend was still breathing. Karen could trace the start of her career to that first meeting. She'd left Barbara's studio—a shared space in a loft building—taken by Barbara's seeming lack of self-doubt despite what clearly had been years without recognition. A sense of self that Karen coveted. For although she'd been a writing major, she'd never had the imagination of her classmates. One teacher even going so far as to suggest Karen consider a career as an editor rather than a writer. It still amazed her how, at Barbara's opening, she'd gotten up the nerve to ask if she could interview her for an article that she would pitch to Art News. Karen's stomach turned waiting for an answer—Barbara towering over her in heels that added inches to her already 5'9" frame. But surprisingly, this formidable woman in her floor length black dress, and tarnished silver spear-like dangling earrings, agreed, but only if Karen promised to learn to write from the artist's perspective. "None of that art critic's bull-shit language! Words made up to make themselves sound smart. They know nothing about art, about the process, how we think, feel, create. If you want to write about my work, then get inside my head and out of yours."

And there it was. She'd done exactly what Barbara had ordered. Hours spent delving into Barbara's psyche. Watching her work through fallow as well as unrestrained periods of creativity. Learning what it took to be committed to one's work. To not accept rejection as failure all the while Barbara questioning every sentence, every thought Karen put to paper. Barbara the consummate devil's advocate.

Eventually Karen learned not to accept every word Barbara uttered as gospel. And over time she was able to apply the lessons learned to other artists' work. She owed Barbara so much. Maybe she had been a leech. But she was a damn good one as Barbara would have to admit. Karen returned to the bedroom.

"You gave me my career, Barb," Karen said as she moved a chair closer to the bed and took Barbara's fleshless hand.

"I did?" Barbara giggled. "What career was that?"

"As a writer."

"And what did you write?"

"About art. Yours, others."

"I made art?"

"Yes."

"And I was good, wasn't I? Very good."

"Yes, and I wrote about it. All of it. Am writing now."

"Really?"

"Really."

"Well good for you."

And with that Barbara squeezed her eyes shut and let out a hiss propelling Karen from her chair and out of the room. Depleted, she gathered up her belongings, told Dee she'd be back later in the week and left. Karen had always assumed—what with their 15-year age difference—that she'd outlive Barbara. But she never expected that Barbara, indomitable Barbara, would take to bed, drifting in and out of consciousness, not to mention reality. Not the woman who had bucked an art world that for years devalued women artists. A world in which even women gallery owners took on only men. The woman who despite rejection after rejection continued to amass an enormous body of work while raising a daughter on her own and working odd jobs to supplement what went for alimony.

Once home Karen's phone beeped. A text from her agent requesting she call him. She ignored it. Couldn't take on his anxiety in addition to her own. This was the first time in all the years she'd missed a deadline. All because Barbara refused to die. "Dear God," she muttered. "Who's the ghoul now?" She sat down on the sofa, her laptop on her thighs. She should send a condolence note to John's wife. Though she wasn't sure it would be appreciated. John had sworn he'd convinced Bethany that Karen was just an old friend, nothing more. But Karen had never been sure Bethany bought it. Better to send the note. Make it appear that's all they were. Dear Bethany, . . . "Oh, for God's sake!" she snapped at herself. "It's time." And it was. Karen could no longer avoid that it hadn't been Barbara's impending death which had held her back. It was her own. Not her physical death. But the coming end of her putting words together on a page. The overwhelming sense that this would be her last book. She put her fingers on the keyboard and typed:

The actual date of Barbara Kaplan's demise is of no import. She died the day she stopped creating art.

And Then There Were . . .

Gerald arrives first. Thin. Wiry. He's sporting a black leather jacket, black jeans, and black shirt—not to mention a shaved head and metro-male stubble. He looks to Jill like someone in the music industry, or a draftsman at an architectural firm. Not exactly her type.

"Caroline isn't here yet," she says as she welcomes him in.

"Just texted that she's caught at the office. Told me to entertain you until she arrives."

She can't tell if he's kidding, his face sort of dead pan. She watches as he drops his leather shoulder bag onto her hall table as if that's where he always leaves it.

"Well, since we're in my home, how about I do the entertaining. What can I get you?"

"Any beer?"

She decides he's wound tight. "If you like Stella."

"Good for me."

"One beer coming up."

He follows her into the kitchen, waves off her offer of a glass, takes the opener from her hand, and wanders back into the living room as she places the snacks she'd prepared onto a tray. He reminds her of her landlord's cat when they first brought him home at 10 weeks of age. He marched—if cats march—around the walls of the entire apartment until he came to the bedroom, intuitively knowing this to be his last stop, Then he climbed up on the bed, walked straight over to the pillows, curled up on one of them and went to sleep. Not that she thought Gerald was going to make his way to her bedroom, even though not her type, she could imagine going to bed with him.

He removes a book from the shelf and begins to leaf through it.

"I've been looking for this," he says. "Can't even find it in the library."

"Oh?"

"You wouldn't mind lending it, would you? I promise I'll return it."

Like hell he will, she thinks. No one returns books. Still, she doesn't want to appear tight, miserly. And it's not as if she had opened the book in Lord knows how long.

"So, I can borrow it?" he asks.

"As long as you return it," she says. The second the words leave her mouth she regrets them. She'll never see the book again.

———————

"Do you still have that book I lent you years ago?" Jill asks Gerald as they sit on opposite sides of Caroline's bed. They are close to running out of conversation. Exhausted from doing nothing. Caroline's dying taking forever.

"Which book?"

"The one I gave you that first night. At my apartment."

"Christ! Haven't looked at it for ages. Do you want it back?"

"You did promise to return it."

"You could have taken it back at any time. You've been in my studio enough times."

He's right of course.

Their nerves have frayed.

———————

She heads back to the kitchen for her drink she'd left on the counter as Gerald's cell goes off. "Yeah? . . . No, I'm here. . . Not again. This is getting. . .Yeah, I'll explain. . . I'll decide. . . I said, I'll decide!" He clicks off, shoves the phone into the back pocket of his pants, takes it out again, turns it off and leaves it on top of the book he'd placed on a side table. "Caroline can't leave the office. Apologizes profusely." His tone anything but apologetic.

"She just texted me as well. I'll cancel our reservation."

"Why?" His annoyance not abating. "We both have to eat, don't we? Let me finish my beer and we'll go."

"You don't have to do that. I'm sure. . ."

"I said we need to eat." He picks up the tray with the snacks and heads into the kitchen.

She tries to stop him. "The reservation is not for another forty-five minutes. I'd planned on drinks here first."

"They'll take us early. If not, we'll sit at the bar."

Caroline never did go for easy.

She barely hears the waiter's list of specials, her eyes on her book now on the chair between them.

"Listen, if you've changed your mind," Gerald says.

"About what?" she says looking up.

"The book."

"No, don't be silly. I offered it. It's yours as long as you return it."

How crazy, she thinks. Why that book of all books should mean so much. One from another lifetime. She'd studied every single drawing, reproducing many until she'd learned every muscle, every tendon, every bone in the body. Well, all right, not like a doctor, but certainly as an artist. Stop! She berates herself. She'd torn that dream to shreds long ago.

"I didn't ask," she says. "Why were you looking for it?"

"Have started to take up drawing and someone recommended it as a good starting point with the figure. But you know that, right? Caroline said you used to be an artist."

"I painted. For many years." Her stomach turns. She just gave away a piece of herself for a hobby. She orders the chicken.

Caroline sighs a shallow breath. One Jill heard often when Caroline was bored. She imagines her saying, 'Enough! Get me out of here.' Caroline is not the patient type—both definitions applicable. A few days before she had opened her eyes, sat bolt upright in the bed and asked, "Am I dead yet?" laid back down returning to her oblivion.

"Why don't you take a break," Jill tells Gerald. "Go home. Freshen up. Sleep if you can." The doc has said death could be a minute or days away.

"Yeah, think I will. Anyway, should check on the dogs. She'd kill me if anything happened to them."

Jill laughs a rueful laugh. "Go! I'm fine. And take your time. I'll call if anything changes."

He packs up his stuff, leans over and whispers in Caroline's ear, gives her a kiss on the forehead, and taps Jill on the shoulder as he leaves.

The rabbi pops his head in the door. An hour ago, it was a priest. Caroline is a lapsed Catholic. Gerald a lapsed Jew. Jill can't get the beginning of a joke out of her mind. A priest and a rabbi walk into a hospice. There's no joke here.

———————

"Sounds like you two had a nice dinner."

Jill can't make out if Caroline is pleased or not. "Missed you."

"I'm going to assume you approve?"

"As long as you do, I do."

"That's not saying anything. You don't?"

"I think we both would have preferred that you were with us. A little crazy having dinner with your new man without you."

"Then you didn't like him."

"Oh, for Christ's sake! He seems perfectly nice. A bit quick to temper, but it appears to evaporate as quickly as it comes. And I am thrilled you found someone that makes you happy, okay?" She's not lying. She wouldn't have chosen him, but then that's true of most of the men her friends have decided upon.

———————

A nurse stops by. One comes in every half hour or so. "You okay?" the nurse asks.

"Fine, thanks," Jill answers.

The nurse checks the IV, changes one of the bags, pulls back the sheet—Jill turns away, privacy still counts although by now she's seen everything. The nurse finishes and leaves.

"I wish you could let me know if you hear me, Caroline. . .Raise a finger. . .Moan. Something. Well, I'm just going to assume you can as they say that hearing is the last thing to go. Maybe if I say something that angers you, you'll come back to life just to give me hell. So how about this? It's all your fault—you getting sick and all. Not to mention making me promise Gerald's next woman is up to your standards, as if I'll have anything to say about it!"

Jill watches Caroline's chest as it continues to move in a slow, shallow, halting motion.

"Come with us to the country this weekend," Caroline says. "It's the only way with our schedules we will ever find time to be together."

"You sure?"

"Gerald will be spending most of his time in the barn. He's really serious about his drawing. Though now he's into colored pencil drawings. Anyway, he'll be occupied, and we can just toodle around."

"Toodle?"

"You know what I mean. C'mon. I've become a colored pencil widow. Need the company. Besides, maybe he will invite you to look. He's planning on bringing them to a gallery."

"Already?"

Caroline shrugs.

How many years before Jill would have even considered taking her work to a gallery?

———————————————

"You two must have been very good friends," the hospice nurse says.

"We still are," Jill responds.

"Of course. Sorry."

"We were in school together. I practically lived at her house. Then separate colleges. She married. Divorced. Then we fell out. It was crazy. She was furious I wouldn't join her in her dad's business. As I said, crazy. Didn't talk for years. Stupid." She stops. Not even sure if she said all this aloud. "Good friends," she says. This time making sure everyone hears.

The nurse smiles and leaves.

"You're really thinking of hiring him?" They're on the screened in porch looking out at the dogs running across the lawn. They remind Jill of Muybridge. Their long poodle legs appearing to be in slow motion as one paw stretches out in front then digging into the ground as the other comes forward. Frame after frame after frame.

"In a way he works for me already. I am his client. So, in reality, he'd just be switching firms."

"Caroline, I don't mean to be crass, but you know what they say about eating where you know what."

"We'll be fine. We've managed so far. Do me a favor?"

"Sure."

"Take a look at his work. Let me know what you think."

"Only if he invites me in." She prays he won't.

The two women spend the rest of the weekend "toodling." Stopping in little shops, walking down to the lake and back, just sitting in the yard, glass of wine in hand, catching up until it is mealtime. It's not until the laundry is done, the beds made up for another weekend, the food that could go bad put into a camper, that Gerald asks Jill to look at his drawings. She looks over at Caroline who has started to puff up the pillows on the couch. She hopes Caroline will say it's too late. That they have to get on the road. But she doesn't. Just, "Go! I need to do one final house check."

"So, what do you think?" Gerald asks after Jill has looked at a few.

"Why colored pencils?"

"Like the control. Again, what do you think?" He's clearly annoyed.

"And you've left the figure? I thought that's why you wanted the book."

"You're not answering, damnit. Never mind, I shouldn't have asked you." He jerks his arm in front of her to gather them up. Clearly, he's hurt. Jill stops him.

"Look! I'm old school. I think they're a damn good start. I'm even a little surprised. But you're only at the beginning of discovering what you can do. I remember sitting in a class so proud of what I'd drawn desperate for the teacher's approval. But when I went up to him, he told me to sit back down. 'I'll look when you've done 1000,' he said. I'd only done 100."

"Did you stay around for the 1000th?"

"I probably left the class at half that. But he did look. Suggested someone else I should work with."

"But you quit."

"After eighteen years. Had to take care of my mom, support myself. I petered out. And I couldn't do it part time. Just didn't have the energy. Anyway, not the point. Go find a teacher whose work you like. Or maybe just a teacher who can teach you something new. Master your craft. Develop your eye. Be harsher on yourself."

Gerald doesn't say a word the entire car ride home.

"Want a break?" Gerald asks when he returns.

"How are the dogs doing?"

"They miss her."

"I bet they do."

"No change?"

Jill shakes her head. "Can't tell. The breathing is so shallow."

Gerald takes his chair. Jill stares at her Fitbit. She should walk. Doing laps around the hall is her new daily exercise. 1000 steps. 2000. 3 . . .

"So, tell me," Caroline demands on the phone the next morning. "He hardly said a word when we got home. Wouldn't discuss it this morning either. What the hell happened?"

"I told him what I thought. That he's got talent. But where he goes from here will all depend on how much work he wants to put in. Nothing wrong if he just wants to keep it as a hobby, but if he wants something more than that, at the very least he's going to have to study."

"Well that should save us a lot of money."

"How?"

"He was going to pay to have them all matted and framed. I owe you one."

"You gave me a weekend away. We're even."

A doctor enters and stands by the bed. "It won't be long," he says.

He knows his stuff. An hour later Jill notices Caroline's chest has stopped moving.

"Gerald," she whispers. His eyes reluctantly leave his book. As much as they both wanted this to end, an ending is the last thing they want.

"He's signed up for a class at the Art Students League." Caroline's voice filled with frustration.

"Good for him." Jill's stomach knots up again. She had done the same years ago.

"It's two nights a week."

"Well, you're usually at work, so what's the problem?"

"No problem, it's just that he's becoming obsessive. Like you were. Art took over your whole life."

"Until it didn't."

"I keep having the feeling that he's doing this to prove something to you."

"To me? Why for heaven's sake?"

"Because you dared him."

"I didn't dare him."

———————

"Do you want to come back to the apartment?" Gerald asks. "I have to walk the dogs."

"I think you should get a dog walker for the next few days." She says. She too doesn't want to be alone.

"Already have. She starts tomorrow."

They are leaving the funeral home. Both surprised at how long it took to make the arrangements.

"We should start making calls," Jill says. "Divide up the list."

They are now in another reality. Numb.

"I can't figure out whether I should sit Shiva?" he says. "Did she say anything to you. It was an off-limits discussion between us."

———————————

"Once I'm gone, he'll have plenty of money to paint full time. He doesn't need to be doing it now."

"He needs a break, sweetie."

"If I'm not getting one, why should he. Hey, want to come with me, Thelma?"

"No thanks, Louise. At least not for the moment."

"You know you can take any of my things you want."

"You'll have to tell Gerald that."

"Can't talk to him about it. He gets too upset."

———————————

Jill is going through Caroline's closet. "What do you think about this?" She holds up a bright red print top and black flowing pants. "I loved her in this."

"Sure." Gerald sits slumped at the edge of the bed.

"Did I tell you that she made me promise I'd keep you from picking the wrong woman. Figured the tuna casseroles would be coming the moment she got buried."

"Not sure she wanted me to find any other woman."

Jill roars. "I think you're right on." Within seconds the tears come. She fights them back. "Listen, when you want to clear out the closet, I can come help."

"Thanks."

Even though the funeral director said they didn't need shoes, she picks up a pair of Manola Blahniks, starts to put them in the bag, thinks better of it and takes them out. Eventually someone could make good use of them. "Gerald, we've got to start calling people. We can say we'll email plans when we know them."

They're waiting for friends to descend. The food is spread out on the dining table. Liquor in the kitchen. It's neither a Shiva nor a wake. No one will be surprised that Jill is acting as hostess. She thinks she should hang a sign up that says, 'no, we are not now, nor have been, nor will we ever sleep together.' Not that the thought hadn't crossed her mind. You don't spend days and nights in a hospital room watching someone ready himself for sleep on a cot without that happening. But she couldn't imagine it. Caroline would always be there between them. Threesomes not her thing.

Gerald arrives. He's put on a few pounds. His metro stubble gone. He has on a new jacket. He no longer carries a shoulder bag. She can't make out his mood as he gives her a perfunctory kiss on the cheek.

"A beer?" she asks.

"Sure," he says following her into the kitchen. "I'm ready to clear out Caroline's closets," he blurts out. "Though think I can do it alone."

"Who is she?" Jill asks not wanting to hear the answer.

"Who?"

"Whom you're seeing."

"How do you know I'm seeing someone?"

"I don't hear from you in weeks. Then you call saying you want to come by and the first thing out of your mouth when you walk in the door is telling me you're ready to get rid of Caroline's clothes. I'm not an idiot. Who is she, Gerald," she demands.

He pauses. "A woman I met in class."

"Is it serious?"

"Very." He's opened the beer. His eyes on hers.

She gives a tight smile and nods her head. "I would like Caroline's emerald earrings," she says. "And my book."

The Bond

Kim would love to take each of the serving forks she's been neatly laying down and ram them into the table as if Harold and whatever the hell her name is were lying there. She can't believe that she's managing to pretend she's okay. As if the only recent shock to her system was Warren dropping dead. And that Vicki hasn't suspected is even more incredible. But then, Vic's head is rightfully elsewhere.

Vicki enters from the kitchen carrying a bowl of fruit every piece meticulously cut. The amount of concentration the slicing took had given her a brief respite from reality. Warren would have said she was a regular Julia Childs—though she's not sure Julia Childs would have bothered. More likely Julia would have chopped, diced and tossed. She places the bowl on the table, picks up the pile of napkins and begins to lay them out like a Japanese fan. She's going mad, she thinks. This is not a party. It's a gathering of mourners. "He's dead," she says aloud, the sound of her own voice surprising her.

"I know, Vic," Kim says. It's the fourth time since she's arrived that Vicki has uttered those words. As if yesterday's funeral hadn't brought the finality of it all home.

Vicki looks over at Kim. Her eyes red. Face drawn. She looks like she's just buried her husband rather than mine, she thinks. Well, it's my husband who died, she wants to say, but holds it in.

"Want to change into another dress?" Kim asks. "You wore that all day yesterday."

"Only black dress I own that's appropriate. Black clothes black clothes everywhere and only one to wear." She starts to laugh hysterically. Then stops. "Sorry," she says.

"To be expected. Want me to fix you a drink?" Kim's been holding off pouring one for herself fearful she'd lose control.

"Have one started—same glass since yesterday. I just keep refilling it. Keep waiting for it to have an effect. But nothing. What time is Harold getting here?"

Just hearing his name causes every muscle in Kim's body to twist into a knot. "I have no idea," she says, trying to soften her tone. She's not lying. She hasn't the vaguest idea if or when he's coming. She prays he doesn't show.

"His eulogy was beautiful."

Kim doesn't say a word. Can't.

"Kim?" Vicki asks. They have been close friends for over ten years. Certainly, long enough to know when the other is holding back.

"What?"

"What's going on?"

"Nothing. Getting a drink. It's got to be 5 somewhere." She wants to kick herself. That's Harold's favorite phrase.

Vicki follows Kim into the kitchen. "Tell me."

Kim's eyes plead with her. "Leave it for now, Vic. You have enough to deal with."

"Oh God!"

"He isn't dying."

"Then?"

Kim wishes the mourners would descend. She doesn't trust herself to hold it together much longer.

Vicki tries again. "Kim, I have enough on my plate. I can't be worrying about you as well. Can't."

Kim takes her time pouring a scotch. Decides she better add some ice. "Where's the ice bucket? You don't want people opening the freezer."

"I've ordered ice to be delivered. It should be here any minute. Stop putting me off. What's going on?" She's surprised how well she's managing. How she ordered the coat rack, the extra chairs, dishes. But then, giving parties was always their forte.

The supreme party givers! This time she keeps the words 'he's gone' to herself. "Kim!"

Kim whirls around. "We've split! Okay? Over and done with. Now leave it for now. Please!" And with that she takes the scotch and heads out of the kitchen. "Going to put on some lipstick. In case he shows, don't want to look like I give a damn."

Vicki leans against the counter. So, Warren was right after all? Why did she argue with him? "I'm sorry, luv," she says as if he can hear her. She hears a man's voice call out to her—the front door left unlocked. "Be right there," she calls back. "Coming!"

It's her next-door neighbors.

"Pastries!" they say. "Where do you want them?"

"Kitchen, thanks," she says avoiding their eyes. Too much pity in them. The wife moves to give her a hug. Here we go, she thinks. The onslaught.

————————

"Do you want to stay here tonight? I can loan you a night-gown," Vicki asks Kim as they put away the last of the food. One more day of this and then slowly people will fade away. A few more weeks and she'll never hear from most of them again. Especially the couples. Husbands hate being with widows. Reminds them of their own mortality.

"Only if you want me to stay!" Kim answers. Part of her wants to go home, the other wants to stay put, to stop time from moving forward.

"I want. Stay."

"Then I'll crash on the sofa. I can run home in the morning to refresh and be back whatever time you'd like."

Finished in the kitchen, they head to the living room.

"Why didn't you tell me?" Vicki says sinking into Warren's chair as if it were his lap.

"I was getting ready to when you called about Warren. No way I could tell you then."

"What happened?"

"He's left." The 'me' left unsaid, obvious. "Had someone on the side for months." Then unable to keep her composure out it poured. "How the hell could I have been so blind? I missed it. Missed all the signs," she pulls a tissue from one of the boxes Vicki had put out on the side tables.

Vicki knows she should go over and give her friend a hug, but she hasn't the energy. "I'm so sorry," she says.

"Quite a pair we are," Kim says. "An aneurysm takes Warren off the golf course and a bitch takes Harold off to her bed. Sorry, didn't mean to compare the two. No comparison."

No, Vicki thinks. There is no comparison. Warren no longer exists. Will never lie next to her. Will never put his arms around her. For all she knows, Harold could come crawling back. No, no comparison. "I wish he had travelled," she says. "You know for business. Gone away weeks or days at a time. Then I could pretend he's off on a trip and will be home soon."

Kim keeps quiet. At least Vicki will have the comfort of knowing Warren didn't leave willingly. That every night when she lies in bed, she will not have an image of him screwing someone else. Kim misses what Vicki says next. Tunes back in at,

"I slept on the sofa last night. Couldn't face an empty bed."

"Do you think you're up to it tonight?" she hopes Vicki won't suggest she sleep next to her.

"My mom slept on my dad's side after he died. Somehow that helped. I'll try that. No, you take the sofa."

Kim begins to take the throw pillows off the sofa. "You know what's really crazy?" she says. I thought we had a great marriage. Well, alright, not great but certainly more than decent."

"Warren didn't think so," Vicki says quietly.

Kim turns and stares at her friend. "What do you mean?"

"We argued about it. Right before he left for golf. I told him he was crazy. Those were my last words to him, Kim. 'You're crazy' my very last words."

Kim's rage peaks. "It would have been nice if he'd said something to me." The minute the words are out, she wants to take them back. "I didn't mean that the way it came out. Just that, do you think he knew Harold had someone on the side?"

"How should I know, Kim. I can't ask him, now can I?" She gets up to get a quilt and pillow. It's the only gesture of solace she can muster.

Kim's eyes follow her friend as she leaves the room. No reason for me to rush back tomorrow, she thinks. Vicki will have plenty of company. Unlike a wife of twenty-five years who has been tossed aside as if she never existed. There are no ritual days of mourning for her.

Mirror Mirror

Joyce woke exhausted. Her night having been spent assiduously erasing name after name, address after address from her old phonebook. She reached for her glasses, stumbled out of bed and, through her morning fog, made her way to the bookshelf in the den. No need to have panicked. It was there, right where it had always been. Still, she couldn't resist taking it down, flipping through its yellowed pages to reassure herself that all the names were exactly as she'd entered them. They were. It had been nothing but a bad dream.

Joyce shook her night's labors off with coffee and the Times crossword—her daily litmus test that her brain still functioned. Then a thorough reading of the Science section, the obits, a scan of the editorials along with the news to see what she'd save for later, finishing with a quick check of possible movies to see. It shocked her how much longer everything seemed to take these days. It used to be that her morning ritual would be complete by 7:30 and now it would most likely be 10:00 or even 10:30 before she'd be ready to bathe and dress. Her outfit, as on most days, a turtleneck sweater, an embroidered vest, a pair of slacks, one of the exotic necklaces she'd collected over the years, and a pair of pendent earrings. Nothing changed from when she worked. She figured that she could leave for her half-hour walk (doctor's orders) by 11 after which she'd return home to freshen up and finally be able to head out to lunch. It couldn't come soon enough.

She got to Le Pain Q early which allowed her a choice of seating. She had her favorites. Any of the tables placed close together along the banquette at the back of the restaurant from where she could look out and watch the other customers filing in. She chose one in the middle of the row. A discernable eagerness playing around her eyes as she waited to see who her lunch companions would be. A few weeks back there had been that delightful young couple who appeared more than happy for her to join their conversation. And before that the two women, only slightly younger than herself, who kept her in the loop all through their meal. Of course, there was always the chance that whoever sat next to her would pull out a book or a cellphone and make it clear that he or she was not to be disturbed. One never could tell.

"What about this one?" she heard a woman say and Joyce broke into a welcoming smile only to watch the woman glance past her and choose to sit two tables away. So, when a woman, likely in her sixties, chose the table to her left, Joyce curtailed her eagerness, simply nodded and returned to staring at the menu allowing the woman time to settle in. From the corner of her eye Joyce could see the woman was impeccably dressed, her hair beautifully coifed—unlike her own that as she used to say had a mind of its own even though it grew out of her head. She was about to compliment the woman on her handbag when the woman turned and much to Joyce's delight, opened the conversation with, "Excuse me, but this is my first time here and I was wondering, could you make a recommendation?"

"Most everything is good," Joyce said, smiling. "Though usually I opt for the turkey tartine. But really, it just depends what you're in the mood for."

"Well if my husband were alive, he died two years ago, he would know what to order. He always did." And before Joyce could extend her belated condolences, the woman continued as if a spigot had been turned on. "He had a heart condition. At least now he's at peace. I'm not. Don't know what to do with myself most days. I live in East Hampton, only come in for doctor appointments. Had one this morning. It's so noisy here, don't you think? I take the Jitney. Too hard now to drive in what with the traffic and . . ."

Joyce didn't know what to do. Clearly the woman was in trouble, but whether this was dementia, severe loneliness, or some specific disorder, she was no longer in a position to do anything about it. She returned to staring at the menu which she knew by heart. There was no way she could engage the couple now seated to her right who were deep in conversation. She considered moving to the communal table, but that would be unnecessarily hurtful.

". . . We used to live in Larchmont," the woman was saying when Joyce tuned back in. "But Kurt, that was my husband's name, Kurt wanted the Hamptons and we moved there. And then he died. Two years ago. If he were here now, he would know what to order . . ."

Joyce had no choice but to motion for the waiter who came over pad in hand expecting her to order. "I am so sorry," she told him. "But I just realized I left my wallet at home. Could you pull the table out so I could get up? Oh, thank you." And with that Joyce stood, gathered her belongings, and squeezed out of the banquet. "Enjoy your lunch," she told the woman. But the woman didn't hear her. She was telling the waiter that she'd have the turkey tartine "like my friend suggested."

"Back so soon, Dr. Whalen?" Joyce's doorman greeted her.

"Forgot my wallet, John. Think I'll just take lunch upstairs today." Silly, she thought, to have continued the lie.

Standing in front of her fridge she settled on a container with leftover tuna salad, grabbed a few crackers and headed to the table where she had set the photograph she needed to take in for reframing. It had hung in her hallway for at least the past ten years clustered amongst the other pictures of family, friends, places visited. Then, last night, as if a poltergeist had invaded her home, wham! down it had come shattering glass all over the floor. A picture of her surrounded by her nine closest friends. Now all but she and Ginny were gone, and Ginny might as well be having moved out of town to be near her daughter. "So where are you all?" She said staring at the faces smiling out at her. "Where the hell are you?"